Hunting the Wild Pineapple

Thea Astley

HUNTING THE
WILD PINEAPPLE

G. P. PUTNAM'S SONS

New York

G. P. Putnam's Sons
Publishers Since 1838
200 Madison Avenue
New York, NY 10016

First American Edition 1991

Library of Congress Cataloging-in-Publication Data

Astley, Thea.
Hunting the wild pineapple / Thea Astley.—1st American ed.
p.   cm.
I. Title.
PR9619.3.A75H8   1990   90-8214 CIP
823—dc20
ISBN 0-399-13561-8

Printed in the United States of America
1   2   3   4   5   6   7   8   9   10

This book is printed on acid-free paper.

Contents

Hunting the Wild Pineapple

1

North:
Some Compass Readings:
Eden

1

Let me draw you a little map.

Take a patch of coastline and its hinterland, put it just north of twenty and one hundred and forty-six east, make it hot and wet and sprinkle it with people who feel they've been forgotten by the rest of the country – and don't really care. Where there aren't hills and unswimmable water, plant cane. There's this largish place called Reeftown on the coast and in the purple hills behind there are smaller towns that grow tobacco and maize and stories that ripen and wither and repeat themselves as cautions against being human. Human! Ah! There's the rub! It's not the dreaming that matters, as the poet man insisted. He couldn't have been more wrong. It's the reality that rubs. And rubs. And rubs.

Everything is very green here. Very blue and very green, and the depth of its coloration whacks out this response, not only from me but from the rest of us, who, having chosen, ripen and wither and repeat ourselves in stories. Which are re-lived by others. Over. Over. Maybe it's only a second-rate Eden with its rain-forest and waterfalls, its mountain-climbing burrower of a railway and sea-bitten rind of coast – a kind of limbo for those who've lost direction and have pitched a last-stand tent.

Take me.

Let me draw you a little map.

Take a failure, male, of middling years, who has already punctured several shiny bubbles. (The soap doesn't really hurt the eyes one little bit after all this time.) Give him thinning blond hair, cut – traditional, a still-bitter schoolboy face, and gently, if you can, remove a leg. There! Easy, wasn't it? This hurt hurts you more than it hurts me. If I say I've learnt to live with it, there'd be something very wrong with my emotional syntax. But you take my meaning. It was a long time ago now, and all those parental plans and daydreams which I, in my orthodox adolescent fever, had intended to shatter were disrupted without my raising a finger. And perhaps for me that was the worst shock of all – the discovery that my rebellion was defused, rendered impotent, before it had truly begun.

Add a name. Leverson. That's right. We met years ago. My parents were a pair of sad marital misfits bound together by the tragedy of me, and although I tried many things to please them I succeeded only in disappointing all of us. Despite 'my little handicap' as I once overheard my mother, Iris, put it, I was all set for a brilliant tertiary career through socio-economics, but when I failed my second year (I am bright but lazy) my mother conceived the notion that it would be nice if I painted, and I spent three spiritless terms in art school—failing to amuse her when I explained that my lack of success was due to my inability to paint with my feet.

I must explain what had always been Iris's problem: she was a kind of artistic *voyeuse*. 'He's such an *interesting* man. He writes,' she said. 'He's such an interesting man. He sings,' she said. 'He's such an interesting man. He acts.' It was *interesting* to write, sing, act, paint, and instantly conferred that especial *cachet* from which I fled to my father's humble and plodding indifference. Not indifference to my plight, for he loved me desperately, but to my success, which he viewed as my simply being; yes, my being, rather than my doing.

I am therefore I succeed. Which is a jolly and heartening piece of philosophy.

After I failed life-class (I always represented the models as having three legs), my ironies being too blatant for stuffy Brisbane Tech., one of my teachers, I discovered, thought me deeply disturbed and insisted on speaking to my parents on the matter.

'I don't think,' the fat chump speculated cautiously to Iris and Bernard, 'that his heart is – er – really in it. Of course the young man has talent but it's not – well, not *preposterous* talent, if you see what I mean.'

'But I thought that was *exactly* what it was,' countered jocular Bernard, and tipped me a huge unsmiling wink.

Mother gave tiny cries of despair.

'Three wasted years!' she was inclined to moan later at unspecified accusing intervals, while Bernard rattled his newspaper busily pretending not to notice behind a barricade of journalistic lies.

Sera comans Iris! The late-blooming. There's nothing like a bit of a classical education.

Prophecy had always played a vigorous part in mother's life. She gorged herself on horoscopes, sported a lucky colour, bought hopeless lottery tickets – it always seemed to be the Ides of March – and patronised endless cup and palm readers who examined dregs or lines and made fatuous forecasts she absorbed like essential food.

After this latest doomsday, unknown to my cynical ageing dad and me, she visited a numerologist who would interpret the signs for sonny boy and steer her (read 'me') in the right direction.

'And what,' asked jaunty Bernard after Iris had been unable to withhold the omens, 'is the gent's prognostication?'

(Mother was always slow to suspect the jibe.)

'Oh, let me tell you! Just let me tell you!'

'Of course I don't come into this.' My scowl seemed wasted, for Iris, who was going through a jet-set phase despite her age, sported what looked like one-way sunglasses and only my mirrored resentment was visible.

'Oh, darling,' she cried. 'Darling! You've the most marvellous number!'

'The formula,' Bernard breathed vaguely, not glancing up from his paper-shield. 'What is the mathematical formula?'

'It was very complicated,' Iris hoped eagerly, 'very. He takes your name, the letters in it, and each has a value, see? Then he adds them all up together with your birthdate –'

'Your cheque account number, insurance policy and car registration –'

'Please! Please! And then he reads off the meaning from the sum of their total.'

'What total?'

'The digits' total.'

'Doesn't he subtract the number he thought of first?'

My laughter socked poor old mother right between the lenses.

She said tartly, 'If you won't be serious –'

'It's rather difficult,' Bernard said, folding his paper and giving me a suffering look.

'Your number's eleven,' unabashed Iris stated. 'Eleven. That's a marvellous number. You have enormous business potential. I know that doesn't seem terribly interesting, but really when you think of our friends who are in that line and are really – well, rather special. . . .' She began listing them.

Bernard yawned.

'You could always wear your number like a footballer, front and back,' he suggested kindly.

Iris began to sob.

Enough of this nonsense. She won.

6

Something called hotel management claimed me after that, and perhaps the possibility of constant engagement with other humans attracted me, for I discovered I enjoyed the excitement of the new face (waiting to crack open its essential humdrummery), the new place. My limp became a kind of bonus attracting elderly lady guests ('Such a nice man!') who were inclined to be forgiving when the service was non-spectacular. In a small way and for a short time I was successful, was sent by the chain I worked for to a variety of overseas New World ritz intended to rub off on my style and consequently theirs, saved small sums of money, watched my parents grow older, greyer, and finally fade before my eyes. It was only after I had buried them that I discovered how much the irritation of my mother had energised me and the sympathy of my father sustained. I planted some late-blooming irises on their graves. I think Bernard would have liked that.

I might as well admit I'm one of those fortunate characters who find even a bus trip an adventure. The stranger-faces across the aisle, in the plaza or the pizza bar, even five rows away in some silent foreign church – for I sometimes extend my hunt within sanctified walls – all flood me with historian's interest as I observe mouths, eyes, hands, breakfast traces on grieving lapels, thick-legged Orinoco patterning of veins, the fluid contours left by expensive private schools and ivy-league privilege. A people-freak, me. And since my particular occupation allowed the indulgence of the vice the vice grew and swamped whatever business virtue I might have had.

My last place of employment for the masters was a pseudo-Tudor *auberge* – there is no other word for its bogus externalia – which the company had established in the heart of grazier country. It was furnished in early Laminex and the hideous conflict between the polystyrene beams with their regular moulded knot-holes and the wipe-down sterility of puke surfaces made for emotional astigmatism.

In any event it was a failure, for the land-owners whizzed overhead in their Beechcrafts and Cessnas as they headed for the nirvanas along the coast, or showered it with the contemptuous dust of their imported limousines. The dining-room remained empty and the bar filled up with boundary-riders and fencers, town clerks and road workers. Apart from occasional benighted travellers, the bedrooms remained empty as well.

When the company auditor on a surprise visit discovered my inertia sprawled in a randomly selected bedroom watching midday cartoons, I was sacked on the spot. So long security! I had, I now realise, been vacuum-packed, and observing the silly spy's eye (they were set so close together he was practically a Cyclops) gleam with malice, I experienced a devastating tenderness for the bucking characters on the screen that kept up their endless quacking right through his outraged tirade.

So here I am watching Crusader Rabbit. To be followed in twenty minutes by the Mutant Lobe from Outer Space. I am thinking of making my own Teev programme called the Deviant Armpit. Yesterday it was Crusader Rabbit and Vampire Lover. Tomorrow ditto and Brutus and the Octopods.

Last month, one half-hour or one lustrum ago – it's all the same in these parts – waiting on the platform at Reeftown for the rail-motor to the tableland, this puffy girl sat beside me and said without preamble (I always like a bit of a preamble), 'Have you found Jesus?' I took it without a quiver. The cane fires had made a lank smoke haze that washed all along the purple bays of the foothills and it was at this I looked as I said no. Turning afterwards, only afterwards, to examine her. She was fatly pretty and her eyes, which had a religious glaze, that awful sobriety of monomania, were slightly mad. But then I am a monopod.

'Look,' she insisted, holding out her scarred wrist for my inspection. Like the Amazon and its tributary system. She must have lost a lot of blood then, though now the lumbering amateurishness of the operation was visible only in a web of white scarring.

'That was before,' she said. 'Before Jesus.' There was no denying the ripeness of her pride, for her present smile, not really shy at the corners, was creamed with sanctifying grace. 'It's different now.'

Hold it! There's this late-night programme I watch sometimes called Good News. Know it? There are these undercooked Yank tycoons injected heavily with social anti-freeze who sit around on vomit and faeces shag-pile, touch each other on the Christian knee, and congratulate each other on their millions.

'There was this flash,' they say. 'There was this power,' they say. 'And the next day I went out and sold sixteen cars, got my promotion, achieved the merger, bought out Firestone, took over Duluth Steel.'

'An' you did that all through the Lord?'

'My, my! Hear that, Jay Ess? Pee Ah?' (SDP? RSVP?) 'All done through the Lord!'

'Notes' Galipo told me once – do you mind if I digress and progress at one and the same time, Sterne-style – that when someone, one of his musical sucking-fish, I suppose, suggested he write a clarinet quintet, all Galipo could say, demurring, was, 'But it's been done before. And, my God, they died soon after!' I can see him now. I'm not looking at the crawler but at his hair-patting reflection in conservatorium office glass. 'Mozart,' Galipo said. 'Mozart. Beethoven. Me. Why die? What's the point?' I suspect he's a mountebank. Have suspected. You can conjugate that verb all ways. But I love that stunning confidence.

This sweet awakening – I mean the uncovering of pretence – is better in a way than sexual arousal, for it excites the hackles, makes me wary of accepting the eye-batting confessions of coffee-table pick-ups, bus-stop amigos and the rest. Perhaps it's my leg brings them on. I'd rather believe it's my Art Rimbaud face, but I guess it's the leg – or lack of it. For I manage my artificial limb so adroitly most people prefer to believe I have been maimed in action, at footie, tested by some paralysing childhood malady, beaten up by thugs with only fleeting interest, and that I am merely manifesting the briefest and politest of limps instead of this devastating mutilation. I kill 'em in bathers!

My phoney foot stuck out in its phoney boot. Its sandalled twin projected beside it. Usually I haul the substitute (this is the real me) back and tuck it out of sight because people get such a shock when they trip over it and there's that unfamiliarity in the contact with flesh that isn't flesh and bone that isn't bone.

I glanced down at the tip of my spurious foot and decided Miss Jesus hadn't seen it yet, was still construing me as a middle-ageing, work-shy body which, inevitably, was moving towards the ecstasies and *longueurs* of the dole queue.

She wanted some comment? Did she? I'm never sure.

Jesus-freaks are so busy with themselves and the saviour it's a one-way dialogue for two. A pity to interrupt. They just have to tell you and keep telling you so they can thank you for the interesting conversation-conversion which they don't really care about. Not fundamentally.

'That's good,' I said. 'Maybe that's what I need.'

'Oh?' she cried at once. 'Jesus!' It was reverent. 'Way out! Way out! Way out!' And I knew immediately she must have come, scarred and puffy, all the way up the coast between communes. 'Jesus is *too much*!' The caftan made her fatter and some tangled beads, the sort we used to pull out of pre-war Easter eggs, vanished in cotton folds. 'I could show you. Really I could. The power! The force!' There genuinely was a lingua franca.

'It's too late for that, I'm afraid,' I said, marvelling at her intrusiveness and suddenly longing for the train.

They're all the same, I'd gathered, though Moth, with the ring through her nose, who would dance to bad flute-playing on sunshiny stretches of main highway while the southern gawper tourists slowed up, had, briefly anyway, held a retreating quality like light. Shadows slide back before sun. She so moved me that once, despite my too many years, I might have followed her, but the bad dream of grocery bills and rates and power and the hideousness of my failed business-man persona were all intolerant.

'No!' she protested, her zealot eyes burning with – believe me – nothing. 'No. Not that. Jesus wants *you*.'

'Not with my overdraft,' I said. But she didn't even wince.

'Oh, he *does*!' she cried. 'He does. Even with that!'

I would have avoided her on the train, but she did the thing I hate most – she helped me. God, I hated her for that, could have irrationally heaved her pillowy stupid body over the Falls. And perhaps she caught the rapid translation in my face

– tightened skin, muscles obtrusive (there's a knot, one of my doctor pals, Maxie Tripp, tells me, forms just below the cheek-bone), so that my protest is visible no matter how the lips compress, or more so. For she was silent beside me. Quirkily envious? I wondered. My scar was greater than hers; humbled the silly bitch.

The train was jammed with homing high-school kids, kicking a treat. Their trannies whined. They spouted bubble-gum carcinomas. They wrenched and wrestled. A munchee-bar culture hatched suddenly about us and in the first whoopee as the train pulled out she fiddled with her beads quite a neurotic bit for a girl who'd found Christ.

'Aren't you rejoicing in my leg?' I shouted nastily, leaning into her hair. It smelt of patchouli.

She said no. In a moment, I thought, she'll ask how it happened.

'How did it happen?' she said humbly to my cocked ear.

'Mundanely. A car. I can't truthfully say I tried to hack it off myself in a moment of despair. Disappointed, eh? No style? Twenty years gone, give or take five years. And now it's safe with Jesus. The leg.'

'In the next life, in the true resurrection,' she assured me fervently, 'we are made all shining and perfect.'

'You mean I'll get it back? But it won't fit!' (This doctor friend who is, in an unobtrusive way, an original, is associated with a group he's formed called Freedom from Teeth. He's an old campaigner with a failing memory who never can recall where he's placed his spare set and for safety keeps them in the sugar jar.) I have a coloured vision of Puffy confronted with the true resurrection after a Tripp dinner and laugh and laugh.

At last she is offended and maintains silence until we reach tunnel seven. 'I used to play tuba,' she confided irrelevantly. Maybe it isn't irrelevant at that. Kids are hooting down loud-hailers made from rolled newspapers. The kids and the tunnel roar together. She seemed an unlikely tuba player. Females making those sub-bottom C sounds! Her cheeks bore little of the muscle drag that goes with brass.

I yelled, 'Were you good at it?'

She looked at me with the terrible candour that being with Jesus gives.

'Very.'

'What's that?'

'I said very. I was very good.' She would tend to become enthusiastic about it? She would. 'I used to play in a youth orchestra down south. I must have been the only girl playing tuba in the country.'

'And you were good?'

'I was good.'

She fidgeted with her beads and did something useless to a swathe or two of Indian cotton.

'Not much opening though. For solo tuba work.'

'Not much.'

We came out of tunnel seven. All the high-school kids had swapped seats and laps. An Abo. boy was hanging half out the door waving and swatting with a handful of brush he'd grabbed as we swept into light. The tinnies were rolling in the aisle. Miss Oom-pah-pah of nineteen seventy – well, never mind the year – hummed sadly.

Never mind the year. This is, I insist, was and will be year one; and not one of us, none of those whom we read of as dead or famous or notorious or lost, none *is*, I say in my best authorised version, but is eternally moving across that stationary screen of stone, iron, bronze, and dollar ages, toting our little ingots and rubber-banded paper piles down through the ages to this, the biggest instalment-paying crowd scene in history. Cecil B. de M., you would be proud.

Far below the train the gorge is evaporating in green light, green into greenness as Lawrence might have said, the early night of rain-forest clambering at the humid, the sharply strategic hillsides. I have only to glance over my shoulder to find the coast still in sun like surprised punctuation. Blue. Yellow. Contrast underscores my isolation and momentarily I think, 'Please take me back into the fold.' Even you, Miss Oom-pah-pah, and I'll toss you friendship titbits, catch yours, act the brisk seal and balance them on my whiskered nose: God help me, so I will.

Tunnel eight. Tunnel nine. Tunnels ten, eleven, twelve.

I am really a monopod self-pitier. No. It's not the leg. Yesterday, I remember – sitting over a loathsome prawn dish swamped in Worcestershire and diverting myself by hunting for visual relief in the boat harbour, the steady pulse of reef waters and shifting masts – I began, dredging from childhood knows where, to intone musically to the other business crustaceans with me: 'In the harbour in the islands in the something seas are the tiny white houses and the orange-trees and daylong nightlong the cool and something breeze of the steady –' They shut me up there, on the brink of my *fortissimo*. And the constriction in chest and throat, a kind of emotional throttling, took me so knottily I had to blow my nose while my eyes slopped with tears I grappled so hard to hold back that my contorted eyes and mouth attracted the horrified attention of a diner at the next table.

'It was up here,' I said on recovery, finger-hanging ten on the table edge, 'that that great sailor waltzed insolently north in his undersized barque. The same year Beethoven was born,' I added, arrogant with a gratuitous piece of cultural call-bird.

'Yup,' they said, the deaf bastards.

And I said, 'But imagine it, will you? Nothing's changed

out there. Those mangroves to the south. The sweep of headland. Forget this bloody little town and you can still see it, that small sailing-ship bouncing north just as . . . .'

They were deaf. Plug-ears. Ah, forget it! It's useless. Where's the sense of history, romance even? I don't think the wide brown land has too much of that. For most of us here it has the visionary impact of a wide brown dollar note. I can't stand, I tell you, not ever, on this palmed and sea-eaten strand without remembering. And seeing. The flying Dutchman of an *Endeavour* caracoles across the scrolls of reef water every time. It makes me bloody howl.

It's the strangers who interest me most. Banks said it was awful up here. So did Cook. But they hadn't met any people.

As I left the restaurant trying not to cough up the residue of prawns espagnole, I leant gently down towards the horrified diner and said, 'Remember the day of judgment. Remember 1770', just to watch the shock on his face. The strangers. Like this Jesus-freak. Like Leo who worked three arrogant weeks as a cook for me at the motel, did body-building, sang vilely, and vanished without trace. Like Mr and Mrs Nameless who, squatting opposite at an arcade pikelet bar in Tobaccotown, admitted that Mr Nameless who was trying to beat the tobacco board, the tea board, with private growings and sales, was being persecuted by artificially induced heart attacks.

'They can do it,' he assured me, sucking taffy tea. 'They measured the pulse-rate of the moon-men, didn't they? Their blood count? All the way from Houston.' He wasn't defensive, just matter of fact. 'Those quacks in Cairns. I've been there. They only have to have a sample of urine, say, or blood. Even a hair, for God's sake, and they've got you taped.'

'Or pus?' I ask.

He ignores me.

'. . . or even a hair sample. Like I say. Just a hair or two, mind you. Then they get their machines homed in on you like radio. Why, I've had three heart attacks in the last two years and before that I was as clean as a whistle.'

You can't scoff at this sort of belief. Maybe the guy's way ahead of his time. But all I'm trying to prove is that you get more magic from strangers.

Tunnels fourteen and fifteen. The magic was running pretty thin here. If only she had her tuba with her. We'd soon be in now and no blow, tubas, blow, set the wild echoes etc., as we rattled along the crest of the Falls gorge. What I'd give for a few sardonic entry snortings as we hit the home run.

'You've somewhere to stay?' I asked.

'Oh, yes,' she said. 'They'll be meeting me further on. I don't get off for a while.'

'Is this all your luggage?' There was a grubby haversack at her feet.

'I don't need much,' she said.

'Not with Jesus.'

'You shouldn't talk that way.'

'It offends?'

'Not me. But some people it might. Some people wouldn't understand. He wants you, you know. Really. But he wants you to find him. You won't believe how your life will change.'

I stood up along with the crashing kids, their bags whacking my indifferent leg.

'Good-bye.' Gravely: 'I could do with a change.'

'Try to find him,' she said, slumped there puffy and untidy in the last of the light.

'He wouldn't want to know me,' I replied and gave her a last nod. Stumping my way through a welter of staghorns and acalyphas I made the steps, made the hill.

The first year, my first year, the place seemed different from anything I had ever known. I would leave it, my private funk-hole, only to be drawn back with the sense of coming home, until finally, after a longer absence, I submit: buy in, rent rooms to car travellers and call myself a motelier. The ultimate failure – and I've failed at a lot of things.

Nothing's changed. There's angle parking by the bottom pub and near the corner store. But that's all. The heavy swags of rain-forest seem as thick as ever and by my private door a weed which I mistakenly watered before the wet last summer has grown twenty feet and threatens with eighteen-inch leaves. To be pressed, suitably, between the pages of some enormous tome. One day, withered, it will drop its brown shadow on the floor, a faded parallel monster of what it parodied.

The wicker lamp-shade is alive with moths, one huge and orange and beautiful as a butterfly in this small golden room, with outside the starting steady hatchet of the rain. Nothing is as horrible as spring and balmy days that make me wretched with their cloudlessness. They animate some fearful antithesis in me so that, missing the heavy noise of river water fifty pounding feet below, I find everything dried up. Especially tears. Humans can't do without those. Again last summer during the monsoons there was one night in the violence of rain when, afraid to sleep in case the whole building collapsed on its jungled slope and crashed crippled with its crippled owner into the flood waters, I switched on all lights, made coffee endlessly, and watched branches rioting outside glass, while between heart-beats and purist sips I pretended courage.

Willy Fourcorners, who lives in a shack just along the road but higher up the ridge, saw my late lights and came tapping on my door. You know Willy by his gentle black earnestness, his big light empty suitcase that he seems to take everywhere. Willy sits with me sometimes and drinks tea. He sat with me all through that night, awkward in his Christian clothing, just as a soother, offering occasional yarns but silence mostly, and staring at the savage landscape from which I've expelled him.

This should really be a separate state. A separate country?

Once in Fixer's cabin, one hour, one year, Fixer and I worked out the new coat of arms – a beer can rampant on a social security form couchant. Do we make it different, the people up here? Fixer and I sit and muse on his tree-mullioned veranda, and if we don't sort it out today there's always tomorrow or next week or next month. There's next year, for that matter. I like it here.

There's the newness of the language, too, in luxuriant sub-cultures filled with Balmain and South Yarra drop-outs who fester in rain-forest patches or on tableland acres. They're lean people and arrogantly young. They groove and they say 'don't heavy-scene me, man' and they despise bread. Not give us this daily variety. They're all for that. There's a great trade in wholemeal and wheat germ in these parts and every dole day you'll see them heading back to the scrub with their government-sponsored goodie boxes jam-packed with the products of a society they reject. I like that, too. I like their cheek. I think of one particular po-faced tick who manages his defence theories on life-style with a base vocabulary that leaves me gasping.

'Vegetables are a superior form of life to humans,' he

decides in the half-built home of one of his friends. We are all slapping at March flies. Kids hob-nob with dogs and sand-piles and delicately balanced timber junk. They'll get round to the house tomorrow, next week, next month. There's always next year. 'You can groove with trees. Man, can you groove!'

I *know* he's intelligent. He used to be in electronics. Now he grows bananas. Or doesn't grow them. He's forty-two and loves heavy rock and moody blues. His teeth buck. 'Who needs bread?' he asks at regular rhetorical intervals. 'It's only funny money.'

'You mean I pay for your chops?'

'Yeah, man. And they taste all the sweeter.'

There's a whole new breed emerging. It's the middle-class struggling back towards the slums and serfdoms out of which they struggled over the last two hundred years. The old *nostalgie de la boue.* In cities they're buying up depressed terrace areas faster than you can blink. A true craving to get back to their economic womb. They're the new urban trendies, so sadly conformist that they are turning their new elysiums into a bedraggled transcription of the suburbia they have been trying to escape. And these ones. They're crawling back to the good earth in their hunt for feudal share-cropping, buying up their starveling five-, ten-, twenty-acre blocks, living with a roof, a tamped earth floor and hessian sides.

I said to him as my stubby turned into a bomb and exploded on one of their unfinished cement stoeps, 'Don't you ever think you're being precious?'

The first year, my first year, they were all there – the Indian tattery, the beards integrated with cranial hair, the jeans that looked urine-stained not only at the crotch, the flute-playing outside the one road-house, the three – well, give them four – chord geniuses of guitar, the lobo-dancing.

Middle-class bums from the south with middle-class accents hitching their way two thousand miles to get a rain-forest high. My office window would watch them come into town, lone characters loping after karma along the Falls road with their tattered knapsacks, looking for the family. Any family would do that first week, the someone who knew someone; and then the newcomer got choosy and moved farther out to the bigger, the more remote, places up in the hills or along the coast to join a pot-happy cluster in some ethnic slum that leaked all through the wet.

The town was crawling with Kombi vans that lurched in from unsurfaced roads to the north, and out of them the kids would saunter to sprawl about the road-house tables. Sometimes one would mooch across unslinging his guitar.

'Can I rip you off for a fag, man?' he asks, the hand already half-way to my pack. 'I'll give you a rain-forest song.'

'I'll give you one not to play,' I say, but he doesn't hear me and he plays six choruses of melancholy while the tourist straights come in for milk or coke or hamburgers and grin at my plight.

Still, I like style. This has style. Fixer has better style.

I've driven Fixer down to Reeftown sometimes and when he's spotted a pretty girl he's leant out of the window of the car and clapped, ever so nicely. He told me once he was in a van with three of his mates, and when they sighted this marvellous sort dawdling along the strand they pulled up and gave her a round of applause. No words. Just applause. 'I used to say congratulations, once,' he said. 'But they took it wrong.'

I wonder sometimes what will happen to these kids at forty, fifty. Already a few of the trendier middle-aged straights around town have made palliative gestures by adopting the patois if not the dress. It's sad watching them jostle the ranks of the ear-ringed lotos-eaters. Lotos-land was certainly what it was in the northern mornings with light hachured between forest and road, a land in which it always certainly seemed afternoon for those casual pilgrimages from one shack to the next, one joint to the next, with the occasional water sounds of plucked strings while the weeds lushed up and over and no one turned a sod. They had had enough of action and of motion, they.

Fixer had done it years before. He was sixty-seven and a natural. Bit worker – roads, fettling, shearers' cook, boundary-rider up in the territory, a touch of fossicking for tin on the Herberton, three years stretcher-bearing in New Guinea, tobacco picking, and at last the pension and a river shack on the rim of Mango, under a tangle of banana thatch and soursops ready to drop. He was a spare fellow, eager as a foxie, with the remains of a good profile and some remnants of grey curl. He read a lot and was a bit of a versifier – doggerel stuff that he dragged out of old exercise-books or crammed into his pockets on the off-chance of finding an ear. They grew to dread him at the pubs. Some of the straights took him up as a curiosity object and regretted it. 'It's like,' Bosie Hackendorf would whisper, 'listening to a hundred Chrissy card verses straight. Why, oh why, did we ask him this time?'

He haunted both worlds. The straights were amused by his hungry vitality, the bawdy confession after four or five whiskies that he loved to screw. The hippies made him for a while their guru, a wonder-man of natural lore, whose knobbed fingers stroked the leaves of plants in growth rituals. Sometimes he'd help them rig up a shelter and then demand payback in beer. He recited endlessly to them things he'd read and remembered, his own terrible verse (they loved it!); and the guitars clunked round the recitative and the joints passed from hand to hand.

Look, this is Fixer's story and I could have begun once upon a time there was Fixer. But there is so much more involved in this degrading love for landscape that has bitten us all.

I must go back a little.

My village spies tell me about Miss Tuba Player of the Slashed Wrists. I'm not sure of her real name. No one is sure óf real names up here. I think they may have said she was called Lilian. Let's call her that. She reached the family. She had been there before in the year or so I was away. She was still *distraite* from the ordeal of finding Jesus, but they welcomed her and in their clumsy way tried to putty the sore patches. A couple of the group were strangers to her, one of them a purple-caftanned pundit who gave out that he was a lecturer in comparative religions from a southern university. (It could well have been glass-blower, I add nastily. The town was full of lecturers and glass-blowers.) He had a voice resonant from being steeped in syllables and the incurious planes of his face emphasised the busybody quality of his remarks. Lilian, disarmed by the philosophic rubble of his little conversational digging motions, wanted him for Jesus. He was not a man to reject any opportunity and it was only a matter of weeks before she wanted him for herself: his plausibility had gentle fingers.

A month before Christmas the commune decided to make a loving gesture towards Fixer, who had spent a week or so plugging their guttering. They held a raffle for him with one of the girls as prize. The bemused winner was Lilian.

She was inclined to sob between her giggles.

'I can't. Really I can't.'

Caftan argued with her – but gently.

'You believe in sharing, don't you? That's the whole concept of this place, isn't it? You do believe in the notion of giving? Well, here is your opportunity to do something loving and generous and absolutely selfless. My little tuba player isn't selfish, is she?'

'But what about you?'

'Oh, my dear, Fixer wouldn't want me!'

'No. You. You and me. You.'

'What about me?' He did whimsical smiles with his head on one side.

'I thought –' she began.

'You thought,' he interrupted gently, 'that I would be proprietorial about this. Didn't you? Don't you see that I must make the gesture, too, no matter how I feel about it? That I'm required to give and it's not only you, my dear. It's me. It's all of us – giving! And perhaps you could –' He paused strategically.

'Perhaps what?'

'Perhaps – look, I hesitate to say this, Lilian, for you know my deep involvements with universal religions – but perhaps you could lead him to Jesus.'

Fixer was Crackerjack Fixer, poor old sod, spry at the parties, pausing only in his elderly flamboyant dancing, as he explained to his partners, because he was becoming too excited. He trudged, cheerful with Christmas, into town along the ridge for his meagre groceries, spaded his banana patch, odd-jobbed for extra grog money about the settlements, and dropped in every so often on the family. They had not yet told him of his luck.

'It must seem natural. Willing. Spontaneous,' Caftan insisted. 'Nothing forced. What's a gift given out of necessity?'

'Like you talk a load of shit, man,' one of the kids said. 'A lay is a lay.'

Caftan had just returned from their jungle dunny. There

was the most tender and innocent damp spot centre-front of his skirt. As the red of annoyance blotched his face, Lilian was flooded with irrational love.

'Oh, he's right! He's right! So right! You simply don't understand a thing he says about Fixer or me or anyone.'

The two of them took their alienation to the pub where they found Fixer drinking by himself at one end of the bar, morose under the thudding of darts on the side veranda.

'What are you drinking?' Caftan asked.

'Brandy,' Fixer said glumly. 'Just brandy, mate, to capture the muse.'

'Elusive, is she?' Caftan was sympathetic as he returned with the drinks.

'What? Oh yeah. The muse.' Fixer looked deep into his glass. 'Not what this'll capture much.'

Caftan remained benign. He lifted his glass. 'Here's to the muse, Fixer,' he said. 'The muse and us. You. Lilian. Me. *Sláinte!*'

'You know the Irish, do you?' Fixer exclaimed, brightening. 'Oh, God, it's ages since I heard the tongue.'

'But you're not Irish, are you?' Caftan asked eagerly. He loved human draggletail.

'"She was jus' the sort of crayture, bhoys, that nature did intend,"' Fixer sang in a trembling tenor, ignoring him. His voice was light and ragged and he kept his eyes fixed on Lilian. A few of the loggers turned round and grinned; on the veranda a fight started round the dart-board and two of the Murris threw punches until the barman thumped them apart. Below in the gorge the mixed goods on its way up the tableland screeched mournfully at the top tunnel.

'I jus' happen,' Fixer announced, stopping his song suddenly and fumbling at his shirt pocket, 'to have brung the muse with me.' He unfolded a dirty piece of exercise-book

onto a brandy puddle. His hands shook a bit, but he cleared
his throat and spat richly through the window.

Caftan leant forward with horrible delight.

'Go on,' he urged. 'Give us the muse.'

Fixer grinned. He read, 'I always puzzle how the turtle
manages to be so fertile.'

Lilian laughed and Caftan said. 'Oh, very good, Fixer.
Very good, mate. But isn't it a bit Ogden Nash, surely?'

Fixer turned sullen.

'It's me own. I wrote it meself. I've published all over
the place, see. Hundreds of poems. Papers. Magazines.
Hundreds. Anyway, that wasn't what I was goin' to read
you. That was jus' one of me little jokes. I'm doin' a sonnet,
see. A sonnet's got fourteen lines. You know what a sonnet
is?'

He didn't really care whether they knew or not. 'Here we
go,' he said.

> *The storm blew down along the northern coast*
> *Just like the storm that broke upon my heart.*
> *A smile, a girl, a glance that made me roast*

(I wanted to say "burn" there, see. More poetic, but it
wouldn't rhyme.)

> *With passion that I thought would never start.*
> *All day the wind and her, all day the rain*
> *Beat on the windows of my house. The trees*
> *Bent over as I did full of the pain*
> *Of knowing that my love would never please.*

'Well, that's half of it. There's a few bits need fixing up but
I've only got six lines to go and she's jake.'

25

'Why, that's great, Fixer!' Caftan said. 'There seems to be a lot of wind and pain, but it's great.'

Fixer looked at him hard for a minute and then raised his glass to Lilian, drunken, courtly, his tobacco-stained teeth bared in a smile of continuing vision. 'Here's lookin' at you, missie.' The half-bow. The lips touched to fingers, the doffing of hat, of heart – well, none of it happened really, but one of the loggers lurched backwards as the barman called 'Time'.

Fixer's drink spattered all over the table.

'Jesus!' he complained. 'An' I hadn't even got the smell of it. Not even the ruddy smell!' All of a sudden, he was tired, old, no longer chipper.

'Never mind, Fixer,' Lilian said gently. 'You just come home with us. We'll get you another drink. Come on. It's lousy here, anyway.'

'That's right, Fixer.' Caftan took his arm lovingly. 'I'll get a little old bottle and we'll take it back with us. More brandy, more muse, hey?'

Under the tulip-trees in the retching dark of closing time they bundled him into the Kombi. Up main street the picture show was still throbbing, the dry-rotted timbers of the building pulsating to gun-play and prairie orchestras. The air smelt of river and the river smelt of jungle.

They decided to take Fixer back to his own place. There had been a birth out at the commune a month before, and despite the fascination of the home-delivery (rain-forest chantings, the washing-down of the baby under the tap at the town garage, the naming ceremony – Wait-a-while) Caftan's proclaimed professional absorption privately craved unshared rest. He had taped some of their joy-cries. 'Like it was a wonderful experience, man!' they kept saying. They had actually said it all through the labour. 'Oh, my God!

Way out, *way out*, man! A great scene! The greatest scene. Like it was way out!' Moth, the mother, had been distressingly limp from a steady nine-month diet of bananas and had to be hospitalised three days after giving birth, while the family accompanied her and, as it were, built them a willow cabin at the hospital gate until the police moved them out. Since Moth's return with Wait-a-while a week ago, no one had slept.

Caftan held forth on these matters as they drove out along the ridge.

'It was a splendid moment, Fixer. The birth and everything about it. But what was really amazing, really opened my eyes, I mean, was the totalitarianism the kids struck when they took Moth down to Reeftown. There's a kind of racism directed at minorities, you know, people like us, people outside the conventional patterns. We're a truly decadent society if we can't accept alternative life-styles. Utterly emptied of generosity or Christian impulse. Well, it hasn't even got to be Christian. A little infusion of Eastern philosophy. . . .'

But no one was listening to him. And no one was listening after they reached Fixer's shack and opened the bottle. Yet after two brandies Lilian gave Caftan what seemed to be a reply.

'You can be a bore,' she said. 'I feel generous.'

'Well, bully for you,' the philosopher replied. He was reaching the nasty stage and when the bottle emptied went out of the lamp-lit shack into the darkness and drove off without the nonsense of good-byes. Lilian had an impulse to go after him, but instead decided to begin the work of apostleship on Fixer who, trembling with grog and poetry and the proximity of this soft pillow of a girl, put a knobbly silencing finger to her lips and simply stared.

'Gawd!' he managed. He grinned. 'Jus' you an' me. I can't walk you back, love. Me old pins wouldn't make it, not at this hour an' with all this horse-piss under me belt.'

She could only nod, nod nod nod, at his old carved face. The raffle, she kept thinking. The raffle.

Obliterated nearly by the thought of what she was about to do, she raised her eyes and inspected him slowly, thoroughly, from his thinning wild locks to his dusty boots, the dying fall, noting the fuzz of hair on his scrubby neck, the blunted energy of his fingers which, stopped now by her silence, paused on the table edge.

'I'll stay,' she said.

He became jaunty as a pup, strutting, leg-flipping, as he moved about the shack, tidying a bit, filling the water-jug, chucking the reeking ash-trays into the night, rinsing the glasses. It was only as he stood in the doorway for a moment, gulping in air weighty with the smells of growth, that he became disturbed by her continuing silence in the room behind him. He turned and saw she had not moved, that her hands were still folded on her lap and that she was bent forward a little as if allaying some inner pain. She regarded him quite steadily and his eyes lost their eagerness and softened. There was no sound but the endless noise of forest and river and the sleep-whimper of his kelpie.

'Hey,' he said softly. 'Hey, you don't have to worry none. I'll roll up in the old blanket. Jus' me an' the muse!'

'I want to stay,' she said firmly and felt the firmness flowing out of her and drowning the room in an enormous power she could not measure. She rose before she could even wonder at it and went across to him and it was as if his eyes could not move away from hers and they stood silently like that for minutes, looking, simply looking, until she saw his slowly fill with tears.

She put her arms round him then and he snuffled a bit and then managed to pull himself into crippled movements that scrambled a makeshift bed together in a corner of the room.

But she stayed the next day too. And the next. And he didn't once read a poem to her and she didn't once speak to him of Jesus. And she told him about her twenty years and he told her about his sixty and on the third day she went to his bed where they made love in a revelatory way for them both. And Fixer fell in love.

During those blurred December days Fixer, shaken within his golden hemisphere by emotion and exertion, travelled forgotten territory whose sunrise zones swam in the trembling light of surprise. His hollow days assumed a solidity on which the imprint of her presence lodged with the most humble of his actions. She cleaned his hut for him and somehow left the impress of her broom like fern in rock, along with the debris of small discarded items that, lost, became part of his most poignant history. He cooked bushman's meals on his primus and stopped going to the pub.

On the fifth day Lilian walked into the township. No one from the family had visited them and she felt that the small cleared grove with its drooping banana-trees had become a deep cistern into which she had dropped without trace. On the way in it rained savagely and quickly and she was soaked through by the time she reached the road-house, her hair and her clothing the second skins that offered no protection. Some of the family were there drinking coffee. A couple played pingpong in the back room where the celluloid ball seemed to tick like a clock. The coffee drinkers tended to drop their eyes upon seeing her and she, dropping her own as she sat at the table with them, saw that the scars upon her wrist stood out with extra sharpness from the wash of rain.

She asked where Caftan was. They were vague. He's

around, they said, but he'd gone down the coast for the day.

'Why?' she persisted.

'Geez, man,' they said, 'don't put it on us. He's just gone down the coast. He's around.'

While she drank her coffee they edged off to the back room and the pingpong and she sat there alone stirring in too much sugar and staring miserably through the flattened bands of her long hair at the empty highway and the sodden sky. Somewhere behind her one of the boys picked out an endless question on his flute, so piercing, so repetitive, that unexpectedly and totally without theatrics she began to weep, the tears flowing steadily and resistlessly down her cheeks while she still stared at the empty road, not bothering to wipe them away at all, just letting their hopeless glitter trickle down into the fruity folds of her neck. Five minutes? Ten? Who knows? Then one of her friends came back to her. Another. Another.

'Don't,' they pleaded. 'Don't do that.' They became charming and tender. They told her he'd gone, he was a con, he wasn't worth even a moment's concern. He had taken off with their only radio, all the spare cash he could find, and most of their books. He was a bum, they said, and she was lucky to know it. She couldn't believe she was lucky. Take your troubles, they advised her, without the least malice in the world, to Jesus.

When she got back to Fixer's shack the rain had stopped and the whole clearing glinted and steamed in sun-slant. He was banging a couple of planks together to make some shelves, but laid down his hammer when he saw her face, swollen and sombre.

'What's up?' he asked. 'You look like you been rainin' too.'

She gave a lying shake of the head, forcing a smile.

'Nothing's up.'

He began getting a meal together, frying up a couple of lumps of steak, stewing coffee. She went outside without offering to help, sat down heavily at the little table in the clearing, and listened to his movements and his whistling. The flute intruded.

When they had finished eating the sun had tipped behind the trees and the trees themselves tipped shadow all over the bush garden, dousing glitter, words. Fixer's kelpie nosed through the late afternoon dream and became only smudged movement where the clearing ended and the forest began. They didn't say much to each other, for words seemed to have lost their lustre as well, and the question Fixer kept tasting at the end of his tongue had an acidic quality that frightened him. He longed (and was afraid to long) to probe the nature of her silence; and he longed too – and was again afraid – to ask her to stay with him, not just tomorrow or next week or next month but next year, for that matter.

His age creaked all through his bones, warningly, and his mottled hand reached over for a twig and snapped it and snapped the halves and then those halves.

'Give us a smile.'

She turned her great mad blue eyes, eyes that seemed to have lost Jesus, on him.

'It won't do, you know.'

'What won't do?'

'This. Just this.'

'You mean coming here? Being here?'

'Not just that.'

'The lovin', then?'

She got his worried smile. Baffled, it was.

'Yes,' she said. 'That.'

'But you was the one,' he said hopelessly, 'as much as me. I mean you was the one.'

'I know,' she said. 'But it won't do.'

'Why? Why won't it bloody do?'

'Because,' she said, 'because I like you.'

She looked down at the veins on his hands, the scrawny heart-breaking skin of his neck, the weathered, alert and suddenly damaged face.

'Oh, I do like you.'

'Well?' old Fixer said. 'Well then?'

'I have to stop it now,' she said firmly. And stood up, shaking grass and leaves and shadow from her long skirt.

He seemed dazed.

'An' I finished that sonnet too,' he said. 'I finished it. An' you've never heard it.'

'I can hear it,' she said. 'Right now I can hear it.'

'Can you?' Fixer asked. 'Can you really?'

'Years ago. I heard it years ago.'

'It's mine,' Fixer said fiercely. 'It's all mine. You couldn't have. I wrote it all.'

'I know that,' she said.

'Then, Jesus,' Fixer cried, 'what the hell do you mean?' – Until he saw she was crying, the grief cutting cruelly at her opened face with all her years running out. 'Come an' live with me,' he pleaded. 'Come on, eh? Just you an' me an' the dog an' this little house an' everything. Eh?'

But already she was turning to walk away.

'No,' she said. 'No.'

That's why I'm here watching humanoids. They're nicer than humans. You really can't beat the old box; and now, so they tell me, they've invented a set that can follow you right around the house. You can't ask more than that, can you?

Humanoids – and vegetables, too. They really are a superior life-form, like the feller said. Even watching Father

32

Rassini praying his way carefully and beautifully through Mass, I'm reminded flippantly of midday matinee!

I hear Fixer went back to the family looking for her and then pleading with her, but the last time he went she was gone. I still watch him trail into town these days with his old string shopping-bag and sometimes he drops in for a yarn; but he never says much and it's as if all the juices had dried up.

2

The Curate Breaker

2

'I like mushrooms', Father F. X. Rassini stated firmly, 'to be under the age of consent.'

With a brief and beautiful gesture of his anointed hands, he flicked his fork, not once glancing at his elderly parent who sat at the other end of the presbytery table. The two curates lowered their eyes.

Old Mr Rassini, who had murky hearing, looked anxiously at his son whose words he had not quite caught but whose critical tone he could assess to the smallest dram of remitting indulgence.

'What's that you say, Father?' His thin old voice vibrated with respect.

'Nothing,' Father Rassini replied, and turning to the curate who sat at his right and lowering his voice he advised confessionally, 'When you have a moment, Father Pike, you really must speak to my father about the shopping. He seems to have only the vaguest ideas about worldly matters.'

Father Rassini was a suave man of God, neither one of the jeans-clad charismatics nor yet a traditionalist, a man who had survived the deliberate humblings of two seminaries with dignity, who believed strongly in the superiority of the clergy, the philosophic inferiority of all laymen, and the non-existence of women except in some cloudily defined area known as auxiliary where he believed them to be tea-makers for God. He allowed occasional guitars within the organ loft, patronised the teaching nuns of his parish ('Stand up for Father, children!' 'Say thank you to Father, children!'), drank only Cointreau with his after-dinner coffee, prayed confidently, and gave cool and semi-political sermons with minatory undertones. That his congregation was eighty per cent female he ignored; that the credibility of most Christian ministers was fast crumbling he did not see. He lived in a kind of eighteenth-century intellectual fantasy of self-conviction whereby any pronouncement he made, whether on the state of the funds of the Holy Name Society (he tended to disregard the Children of Mary: though he paid enormous overt respect to Christ's mother, he shelved all others), the annual parish fête, or the celibacy of the clergy, had more than a touch of the old *ex cathedra*. Healthy young curates became limp sweaters in his presence. He first-named (by priestly privilege) all parishioners he met within the first moments of introduction and did not appear to hear any similar address to himself. He played mid-week golf, drove a large Mercedes that had been given him by his late mother, visited only the influential of his parish (curates dealt with needy cases: they had no powers, but their timid reassurances bred comfort), and became extremely active on diocese committees that entailed his leaving the parish for decision-making.

As a godly man he was inclined to think big.

After his mother died, he was presented with a terrible problem. For years his apostolate had been in the north of the country. He had endured the rigours of the north-west for ten years in the tiny parish of Flystrike, spent another five on the sugar coast, and had come finally to his reward in the large and wealthy parish of Tobaccotown. His only brother and sister chose to live in colder states to which his father stubbornly refused to go. When his odd-job man and house-keeper gave notice within a week of each other, the problem of his father seemed to be solved, as well as that of having to pay even the sub-union wages he gave to those privileged to serve.

'I think,' he suggested in an attempt at concern for the old man on one of his rare visits to his home town, 'I think you had better come and live with me.' The old man, who was a fairly active seventy, glanced away from the roaring television to mumble, 'What's that you say, Father?' He had all his ancestry's insane respect for the cloth.

Father Rassini moved across to the television and lowered the volume.

'I think,' he repeated more loudly and firmly, 'that it would be best if you came to live with me. It's not an uncommon thing, you know, for the clergy to have their parents with them. Especially at those times when –' He began to trail. 'What I mean is, we can't have you languishing here, now can we?'

His father gave him a sly look.

'I'm not really languishing.'

'Well . . . no.' Father Rassini did a thoughtful fingertips together. They were beautiful fingers, pale and well-formed, and they had never struck one domestic blow in anger. 'Not languishing. I chose the wrong word. I'm concerned about you. I want to keep an eye on you, make sure you're well. That sort of thing.'

The old man shoved his tea-cup to one side, picked up the teapot and shook it back and forth.

'Stirs up the tannin. Just what I need. Must have some little vices.'

'That's exactly what you don't need,' his son said irritably.

39

'The tannin is extremely bad for your liver. You'll simply have to come back with me and I'll watch your diet, make sure you eat properly. I will,' he added, trying whimsicality, 'draw up some dietary commandments!'

The old man refilled his cup and drank thoughtfully.

'What's happened to the telly?' he asked plaintively. 'I can't hear it.'

Father Rassini sighed. 'Please . . . please,' he said. 'You must give this some serious thought.'

'Now, now, Father,' the old man said, watching his son over the cup rim as he drank, 'I'd never fit in there. Not with all those other Fathers. I'd be a nuisance.'

'What nonsense!' Father Rassini became sprightly. 'Nonsense! I simply won't have you talk such nonsense!' He gave the confessional smile he reserved for cases of scruples. His jaws throbbed. 'Why, you could give a little hand now and then. Just a little hand. Answer the phone for me. Take messages and so on. Keep an eye on the church when we're all out. That sort of thing. My word I'll keep you up to your regular duties, won't I? No dodging those Holy Days of Obligation!' He laughed rather too heartily and his father was inclined to sulk.

The old man's protests went on and on over five visits. Five visits to capitulation, and suddenly it became easier than he had believed to install the old man in a spare room at the back of the presbytery and fit it out with a few oddments from the family home now up for sale. The double bed? Father Rassini thought no. The old desk? Perhaps. (Would it look like psychological rivalry?) The best of the easy chairs? But of course of course of course! The jocular *absolvo te*.

Funnily enough the old man slipped into the course of presbytery life as easily as a fish and the curates watched with fascination as Father Rassini gradually bestowed one domestic chore after another on him. He was a fair plain cook, having lived alone for a couple of years, and the old clerkly skills he brought from forty years' humble nine-to-fiving in the public service manipulated the parish accounts. After a year Father Rassini decided it was the best move he had ever made, and even practised small criticisms that he felt would strengthen his parent's grip on grace. *Per minutias ad coelum*!

There was living not far from him in the same country town an Anglican canon called Morrow, a fierce anti-papist who was as filled with splenetic loathing for what he called the 'incense pack' as the other was with the total indifference of infallibility. As much as was possible in a town that size, these two avoided each other, though it was inevitable they should meet at municipal junkets where the local council solved squabbles over precedence by allowing each cleric in turn to have the position of vantage.

Canon Morrow was married to a humble little woman he had saved from a diocesan typing pool many years ago. Their union was fruitless in every way and she had become absorbed, though in a very minor capacity, by parish duties through which her unobtrusive form wavered like a jumble-stall wraith. 'The Canon' she always called him, modestly but with terrified pride when she talked with her few acquaintances – they were only that; for her husband despised anything as passionate as friendship. And he puff-facedly accepted her diffident worship, hardly seeing her, certainly never listening to her, and only occasionally touching her.

'I am afraid,' Father Rassini would announce, smiling to his smiling curates, 'that Mrs Morrow in choosing marriage to the Canon has made a far greater sacrifice than we in choosing celibacy.'

The two men used to go one day a week to give religious instruction at Finecut High School. Although Father Rassini felt this to be a duty he could hand over to one of the curates, he sensed the subtle flow of by-products from a genial public appearance and retained this particular office for himself.

'The careless . . . the carefree, shall we say? . . . I mean those who take their spiritual obligations lightly . . . need perhaps a more practised hand on the reins.' He would explain this delicately to the curates, sipping his Cointreau, wielding the pause, flick flick flick, with such conviction the vintners knew exactly where they stood in relation to the grapes.

Except for the briefest of all possible nods as they passed in some chalky corridor, Canon Morrow and Father Rassini had not spoken for years. Those townsfolk whom the canon knew positively to be papists he cut dead.

'I believe,' he once accused the history mistress at Finecut who also happened to be one of his flock, 'that you married a Roman.'

'Oh, no, Canon Morrow,' she replied coldly, 'I married an Australian.'

His bigotry became a legend and a joky one at that. On St Patrick's Day his class would greet him with silent shamrocks pinned to their school blazers or confront his wowserism at other times with AA badges or White Horse symbols above which their bland morning faces shone with . . . something. Still, there was this token nod to Father Rassini, a kind of grudging acknowledgment that they were both professional men of God, though the Canon believed quite firmly that his God was different.

Not long after Father Rassini's father had come to live at the presbytery, Canon Morrow was subjected to a type of earthly purgatory by a pupil called Fabio Galipo. Fabio was sixteen, subtly clever and sombrely good-looking, with a rare skill for engendering a distemper, of sorts, in all his classes. Not that he was ever observed flinging the spit-bomb, toppling the desk, inscribing the *graffito*; but where he was there too were these things. He lived at ease within the eye of the storm while about him the furies he aroused by his gnostic style raged.

At the beginning of second term he quietly absented himself from Father Rassini's instruction class and slid unobtrusively, grave and handsome, into the group of sixty Anglicans Canon Morrow was haranguing in the school hall. The group quivered with expectation.

Outside the rectory Canon Morrow's disciplinary powers were inconsiderable. He cut a booming figure in the pulpit, but his authority could not circumvent yawns, even snores; with adolescents he was hopeless and his exasperation only fed the giggles and talk that fragmented the message. This particular morning it was the unusual quiet that alerted him.

Glancing towards the back of the group he noticed a vivid face riveted – riveted? he asked himself – upon him.

He continued to drone. '"If any man among you seem to be religious and bridleth not his tongue, but deceiveth his own heart, this man's religion is in vain." Epistles. James one. Verse twenty-six. Quiet down the back, please. And again, and I draw from St John the Divine: "He that is unjust, let him be unjust still: and he which is filthy,"' (here he began a vile crescendo) '"let him be filthy still!" You know, of course, that I refer, dear children, to the evil forces of papistry that are among us. To the perpetuation of lies. To the deliberate misinterpretations of God's holy word. To the conniving, to the deceits that are wrought upon those misguided souls who compound their errors by communion in a church which has always borne false witness. Get out the boy who made that noise! "But the souls of the righteous" – and I am quoting here from Solomon, and Solomon was surely the wisest man who lived – "the souls of the righteous are in the hand of God, and there shall no torment touch them. In the sight of the unwise" – note that, "unwise" – "they seemed to die: and their departure is taken for misery, and their going from us to be utter destruction: but . . ." ' He paused and then roared, ' "THEY – ARE – IN –PEACE!" ' '

A hand flapped at the back of the hall.

'We,' continued the Canon, ignoring the waving fingers, 'fortunate in our church, our creed, our Anglican sentiments, we, too, are in peace. We –'

'Sir?'

The Canon glared at the flapping hand.

'Yes. What is it?'

'Sir? Wouldn't it be better if you told us more positive things? I mean about Anglican dogma, sir. You know, doctrine and stuff, instead of spending the time telling us what's wrong with the Catholics.'

Rapt, sixty-one pairs of eyes gloated on the Canon eagerly.

He flushed heavily red.

'Stand up, lad.'

'Sir?'

'I said stand up!'

Galipo rose smartly and gave a warm ingenuous smile of breath-taking candour. 'Sir?'

'You're new, aren't you?'

'No, sir.' Someone tittered.

'You know what I mean. New to this class, boy?'

Galipo dropped his eyes a moment as if he were pondering the exactness of this.

'Not to the class, sir,' he offered finally and politely. 'I know all the class, sir.' The Canon could feel the vibrations of totally silent mirth. 'But I suppose I am new to you.'

'What is your name, boy?'

'Galipo, sir.'

'And why haven't I seen you before? Why haven't you enrolled in this class in the regular way?'

'Is there a regular way, sir?'

The hall shouted with laughter. Galipo looked confused and guileless. The Canon's mouth worked but no words came. 'He was speaking faster than sound,' Galipo explained later.

'Sir,' he went on, 'conscience knows no regular way. I am a convert.'

The Canon blinked. 'From what?'

'From papistry, sir,' Galipo explained earnestly. 'I have seen the error of papistry.'

The hall leant forward in delighted anticipation.

'You mean you were a Roman Catholic?'

'Yes, sir.'

'And you have decided to join this religious group?'

'Yes, sir.'

'And your parents, may I ask, are they aware of this step?'

Galipo smiled and then became solemn. The Canon waited.

'We never discuss religion at home, sir. My father says I must decide for myself.'

'This is a grave step,' the Canon said. Again he thought he felt but could not see the vibrations of laughter. 'Are you perfectly sincere?'

'Perfectly, sir,' Galipo lowered his eyes. 'I acted only after mature judgment. I felt' – he hesitated nicely – 'that somehow the – er – superstitious element of Father Rassini's classes, sir, if I may say so, had an insincerity fatal to the Christian principle.'

He raised his limpid eyes and looked frankly at the Canon. The hall hugged itself.

'I see.' Canon Morrow was bemused. But the boy seemed

genuine enough. Not like that other rabble. He felt flattered, too, by the clarity of the dark eyes gazing simply into his. 'Yes. I see. Well, my boy,' – here Galipo gave a smile of pure radiance – 'we must each find God in our own way. We can rejoice that you have come at last to the one true Church. But I do think you had better speak to Father Rassini about this.'

'Oh, I wouldn't like to do that, sir,' Galipo replied gently. 'I would hate to offend him!'

The Canon nodded several times. What delicacy! 'Of course, of course. Well. . . .' He tried to repress his triumph. 'You might wish to come to me privately about this.'

'Thank you, sir,' Galipo said.

The Canon went back to the rectory thoughtfully and made some inquiries about Fabio Galipo which told him little except that the boy's father was a failed musician-cum-lawyer who had set up practice in the town a year ago, that there were three children, and that Lawyer Galipo was very wealthy. He liked that. His feelings of victorious clerkship were so vigorous he actually spoke once or twice to his wife during lunch and, though he ignored her replies, she felt stronger too.

When, the next week, he passed Father Rassini in the school grounds, he offered him a short good-morning sprung from an uncharitable flush of victory. One down, he thought, and rolled over through the heavenly shadows of the pepper-trees to the school hall and his class.

Which he opened with prayer. He prayed resoundingly and fruitily, rolling his reverential clichés together with tremendous ardour. The spontaneous mode, he thought, was really his. At the back of the room he could see Galipo sitting with shadowed face and once again he felt the victor's surge and his voice, ripened with the juices of evangelism, hooted its confirmations more resonantly. Yet the quietness of the class was disconcerting to one used to chaos. Briefly he wondered about this, but decided it was gentle rain from heaven, unclogged after months, but unclogged.

The half-hour drew to its close.

'Have you any questions?' Canon Morrow inquired.

Galipo raised his hand.

'Well?' The lad had not yet visited him privately for instruction. The Canon put that down to the irresponsibility of youth. He frowned.

'Sir, it's not quite relevant, sir, to what you've been saying this morning. . . .'

'Come along, lad, come along.'

'Well, sir, while I reject, as I told you, the infallibility of the Pope, it does strike me –' He did hand-wobbles of confusion.

'What strikes you?'

'Well, sir, there does seem to be a pretty dogmatic line here, too. I mean, who makes the directives?'

'I beg your pardon?'

'Who lays down the law for Anglicans?'

'You put that rather unfortunately, lad,' the Canon said. He launched his eyes upward. 'God does.'

'But I thought the Archbishop of Canterbury was head of the Church of England.'

'The temporal head.'

'Then isn't that much the same thing? As having a Pope, I mean.'

'Not for a moment,' the Canon replied irritably. 'Our Archbishop makes no claims to infallibility.'

'But what he says goes?'

The class started to giggle.

'You do put it crudely, my boy,' the Canon replied. 'But fundamentally, fundamentally – yes.'

'Then he's responsible for church laws on divorce, say?'

'Are you contemplating such a step?' the Canon asked with unexpected humour. The room roared. Pleased with himself and over-playing it, the Canon boomed suddenly, '"Whosoever putteth away his wife and taketh another, committeth adultery!" God made that law.'

'Oh, I know that, sir,' Galipo interrupted. 'That's what Father Rassini said. But Anglican prelates insist their laws are God's laws, then?'

'They are. They are, indeed. Through the interpretation of Holy Scripture.'

'Then, sir,' Galipo asked, his face bland, questing, 'what about the Judaic proscriptions on women at – well, at certain times, sir? Do Anglicans insist on those?'

Some of the bigger boys began nudging and sniggering. Everyone watched the Canon's outraged face with joy.

I hate you, boy, thought the Canon unexpectedly. I truly hate you.

'That was purely,' he said slowly and with awful emphasis, 'a social convention of the times and not dogma, not an article of faith.'

'But, sir,' Galipo persisted maddeningly, 'how do we decide which is revealed truth and which is merely social convention?'

'The Church leaders in their wisdom decide.'

'But that *is* like the Pope, sir, if you'll excuse me. Couldn't they be wrong sometimes? I mean if *all* the Bible is revealed truth surely we're obliged to follow all its beliefs.'

'Sit down, boy,' Canon Morrow said.

'But sir –'

'Sit down!'

'Sir,' Galipo said politely and lowered his head. And smiled.

Canon Morrow drove home from his morning's

apostleship in fury. His profiled dignity ignored landscape orisons, loops of summer wind, the peculiar dispensations of green and pungent trees. He was immune to the nostalgia of horizons that slid past his office-jobbing for the Lord and only once or twice in his boyhood years, triggered by some special combination of sounds or the tantalising perspectives of avenues, had he ever imagined departures of the spirit. He tried to calm himself by concentrating on his world: two slices of ham delight for lunch, the weekly preparation of the Sunday sermon, the baptising, the marrying and the burying of names he would enter, zealously detailed, in the parish register.

That boy, he thought. That *boy*!

'Sir,' Galipo announced the next week at discussion time, 'I have tried to persuade my father to apply Judaic strictures to mother.'

The Canon felt a choking sensation.

'You what?'

'My father says it is domestically impossible unless we build on.'

The class roared.

'O Almighty God,' intoned Canon Morrow moving straight into prayer, 'O Thou who has created great and small, rich and poor, the weak and the strong, vouchsafe unto the least of us the benefits of humility. Purge us of our pride. Teach us to accept, not to question. Teach us to serve, not to lead –'

'But, sir!' Galipo interrupted at that point.

'– to believe above all,' the Canon blared, 'in those whom Thou hast appointed as Thy humble ministers.'

The class bowed its head on its laughter and Galipo, glancing once more with terrible and artless appeal at the blind-eyed Canon, lowered his head also.

Father Rassini had had a bad fortnight. A week before Father Pike had borrowed the Mercedes and wrecked it in an encounter with a grader on the coast highway. Only Father Pike had been spared. The other priest, Father Watters, had been sent on supply for a month to a mission settlement on the Gulf. For once in years the ladies' auxiliary had failed him: flowers on the altar withered and the candlesticks were unpolished. And now the cutlets were overdone.

He commented on this to his father, briefly but bitterly. The old man gave a dry-bones, unoffendable smile. He hadn't heard. 'Dear God!' Father Rassini murmured and went out into the garden where he placated himself by wandering beneath the mango-trees, absorbing their gravity into an inner spot of calm that he felt expand through the trembling itches of his blood. He lit one of the ten cigarettes he permitted himself each day, inhaled, sensed the exasperation subside and then noticed that the vegetable patch had been unweeded for weeks.

On his next visit to the school Father Rassini became aware of Galipo's absence.

'Father!' the class cried eagerly to his inquiries. 'Father, he's joined the Protties!'

'He's what?'

There were monstrous quacks of pleasure.

'One at a time, please,' Father Rassini bellowed. 'One – at – a – time!'

'He's gone to Church of England, Father.'

'He's renounced the Pope.'

'He's asked Canon Morrow to receive him.'

'You are joking,' Father Rassini said faintly.

They fell over themselves disabusing him. They assumed spurious expressions of moral outrage.

Father Rassini restored order with a shallow wave of his beautiful hands.

'Please!' he said. He paused. His lips tensed. 'While, my dear boys, we must not reject the freedom of the individual conscience, we must pray for those who are misguided. To cut oneself off voluntarily from the holy body of the Church is a matter almost too horrible to contemplate.' He stopped to contemplate it. The faces before him registered horror. 'Apostasy, my dear children, is a grave matter. A very grave matter.'

He repeated those words at dinner that night. His father glanced down the table from the vegetables he was doling out.

'You like pumpkin, Father,' he said. 'Like some more, then? Got it cheap by buying a job lot.'

Father Rassini knew a spasm of fury.

'I am speaking,' he went on petulantly, turning to Father Pike, 'of one of our flock in deadly peril of losing his immortal soul.'

'To whom, Father?' the junior curate asked respectfully. 'Not that fast piece of the Corkerys?'

'Really!' Father Rassini snapped. 'This is not a matter for flippancy.' He took a recuperative wine-gulp and worked at his plate for a while. 'This steak is really dreadfully tough,' he announced, raising his voice, 'dreadfully, dreadfully tough.'

The old man looked up. 'I'm sorry, Father,' he said. His son didn't look at him. 'Best I could get. They take down old codgers like me, you know.'

'Well, you must say it's for the presbytery. Did you say that? It's a bad best. A bad best. A man can't be expected to carry out his duties on a stomach filled with leather.'

'Things of the flesh,' Father Pike muttered in soft rage.

'Oh, how you harp on things of the flesh.' He added loudly to the old man, 'It's very nice. Very tasty, Mr Rassini.'

'Father Pike,' Father Rassini said coldly, 'you have already incommoded me this month. I am without a car. Kindly allow me to attend to the running of this presbytery in my own way. You show not the slightest interest in a matter that should really concern you, that of a soul in peril. All you can do is make flippant and intrusive remarks. As you appear to have no concern at all for the well-being of our own parishioners, I will attend to the matter myself. You seem doomed to create chaos.'

Father Rassini brooded all that week, his congested and swollen notions emerging as testy directions to Father Pike and the old man; but while Father Pike sulked, Mr Rassini, vaguely frightened by what he felt to be general displeasure, tended to keep to his bedroom at the back of the presbytery where he twiddled with his short-wave radio. One evening late as Father Rassini was finishing the reading of his office, the blurting and rending static seemed to scrape his mind raw. With an infuriated marker-finger whacked into his breviary, he galloped down the midnight hallway into a cube of naked bulb-light and jungle noise.

The old man sat sideways to him with an absorbed and distracted smile of ancient pleasure.

'The time!' Father Rassini shouted. 'The time! Have you any notion what hour this is!'

The old man neither heard nor saw him.

Father Rassini crossed the room and bending down shouted directly into the old man's ear. 'Turn – that – thing – off!'

Heart-shock knocked the old boy. Snorting sideways with the fright of it – a son whose foreign eyes he could never have sired – , he began a shaking fumble at the switches.

'Sorry, Father,' he creaked. 'I'll keep it down, eh? I was just getting Tokyo,' he added hopefully.

'I want . . .,' Father Rassini began, but something ruptured in the old man's posture skittled his protest. A bruising somewhere? The sudden slump in sound had extended to shoulders, mouth, like parody; and when he repeated, 'I think I was getting Japan', Father Rassini bit ferociously at his gobbling lips and padded back to his wasteland and breviary where he discovered that he had lost his place.

Next morning in the mush of the first summer wet, he borrowed Father Pike's bicycle and wobbled across town to the Anglican rectory. Passing trucks made repeated and unspeakable assaults upon his black alpaca. The ends of his trousers dangled wet and muddy. After he had propped the bike by the veranda steps he stood for a minute in the porch shelter and mopped off his soaking neck and face as if he were rejecting baptism. He kept willing himself to be calm. Level with his eyes, the door-knocker, buffed to fanatic brilliance, staring blandly back, gave him a shrunken and distorted simulacrum of his priestly rage.

Canon Morrow opened the door and there was a small moment of stupefaction.

At last Father Rassini, swivelling about for suitable clauses, ungummed his tongue.

'Forgive my intruding.'

The Canon was busy with stratagems. He remained silent.

'Look, I do apologise for calling this way but there's something I must –'

'Come in,' the Canon said shortly. 'Take that coat off. You'll drip all over the hall.' He found he was breathing silkily as he held the door back.

Father Rassini stepped onto a blaze of linoleum across whose skitter width two family groups behind glass inspected each other for signs of weakness. A table stood exactly half-way along the passage and on the table rested a bowl in which four flowers floated equidistant. A Bible lay beside the bowl. There was a kind of humming silence through which the chatter of rain upon the roof intruded, Father Rassini thought erratically, like a gauche conversationalist.

'This way,' Canon Morrow said.

His study also gleamed. There were two walls of books that appeared unthumbed but dusted, an important desk with a lot of conviction about it in its geometrically precise arrangement of papers and a couple of easy chairs. Only one looked sat-in.

'My little castle! My – er – holy of holies!' The Canon uttered an ecclesiastic two-note laugh of self-mockery. 'We shan't be disturbed.' He dropped heavily into a chair before his guest and crossed potty legs. 'Now. What can I do for you?'

Uncomfortably Father Rassini shifted his wet feet about on a carpet the colour of scrupulous lamentation. Rain still clobbered the roof.

'It's a delicate matter,' he began. He disliked the way the Canon was squinting across the metal-gleam perfection of his desk. 'It's about one of the students.'

'Indeed! Who?' the Canon asked maliciously.

'Young Fabio Galipo.' Discharged, Father Rassini cleared his throat and decided to wait.

'What about him?'

'Well, he's absenting himself from my classes' – taking the plunge – 'and you must understand the boy is one of my parishioners. There's some story going about – absurd, I'm sure – that he's taking instruction from you.'

'Not absurd,' the Canon said, translating satisfaction into a pudged jaw-set.

'Not what?'

'The story,' Canon Morrow stated with vindictive slowness, 'is not absurd. The boy came to me voluntarily.'

Despite the steady chug of a ceiling fan that chopped the air into slow segments, it was hot in the study. Father Rassini dabbed at some sweat.

'But of course! Of course! I was not suggesting there was any coercion.'

'Pardon me, Father Rassini, I resent even the use of that word. Even the word. Yes. I resent it.'

Through an atrocious gulping emotion in his throat, Father Rassini managed to switch in his turn to urbane interrogation.

'Word?'

'Coercion.'

'Oh, I see. I see what you mean. No, not quite that. What I'm trying to say, Canon Morrow, is that I realise no pressure was brought to bear upon the lad. He can be a difficult boy, as I'm sure you've discovered.'

'Not at all. Not at all. A charming boy,' the Canon said coolly.

'However,' Father Rassini continued, ignoring him, 'what we must consider is how to handle the situation without creating – er – scandal.'

'Dear me,' the Canon said. 'I hardly imagine the conversion of a soul to the Anglican communion a cause for scandal. In fact, I find that equally offensive.'

They wrestled each other with stares and silence until Father Rassini regained a bogus calm.

'Try to understand, Canon Morrow –' How offensive that

full title is! he thought. 'Try to understand, Canon Morrow, that regarding ourselves as we do as members of the one true faith is a fact that poses problems for the Catholic community here and for the boy's family as well. This is a small town.'

'Good heavens!' the Canon cried. 'I cannot debate the lad's spiritual position with you. He has chosen. He has come. Is that not enough?'

'Not quite,' Father Rassini insisted.

There was a soft tapping at the door.

The Canon ignored it.

'What do you mean?'

'I mean the boy's a trouble-maker.'

'Are you implying I am unable to gauge sincerity?' the Canon demanded. He went a tricky colour.

The tapping was repeated and cautiously, very cautiously, like a film trapped in slow motion, the door opened a fraction. Father Rassini watched fascinated as the Canon's wife put her tentative face apologetically round its edge.

'Excuse me, dear,' she whispered.

The Canon went on talking, his voice raised and inclined to babble. 'Do you really mean to say, Father Rassini, that I am incapable of assessing the genuineness of a soul in search of the true faith? That I cannot recognise veracity, candour, the authentic?' He could feel the words flowing out of him like tongues. He went on and on. It was Pentecostal, Father Rassini decided, giving him grudging credit. Absolutely Pentecostal.

'Excuse me, John,' his wife interrupted once more. 'Please could you –'

'What?' the Canon shouted, swinging to face her. 'What do you want, woman? Interrupting me like this!'

As Father Rassini watched she seemed to wither before his eyes, hers bulging with a sudden surge of unshed tears. One half of her mouth, deformed, gave him a little smile like a social tic. She began to say, 'There's something the matter with –'

But the Canon roared, 'Come in! Come in, woman, and shut the door. You know I've told you over and over, never, not ever, to disturb me when I'm on parish business. Haven't I? Haven't I?'

She stood there quivering, thin, neat in her ten years' dated dress that hung limply and with apology upon her, and appalled.

'Yes,' she whispered.

Father Rassini's attempt to rise was caught in the slips by the Canon's insane eye. 'Sit!' he commanded, not bothering to look. He could concentrate on nothing but his unfortunate wife, noting with fury that her bun was coming undone. His mouth filled with saliva.

'This – must – not – happen – again!'

The room took on a crystal tension that transferred a glaze of rage to the Canon's eyes, a rage he could no longer control as the second assault, the sloppy coiffure, guyed his dignity.

'Kneel down!'

His wife blinked unbelieving and fearful eyes.

'I said kneel down!'

'Please,' she whispered. Appearing to shrivel.

Furiously the Canon indicated the floor.

'Down! Kneel down, woman, and repeat after me these words for forgiveness.'

Rigid on his probationary chair Father Rassini thought, 'Oh, my God my God.'

'Please, John' she begged again, so softly it could hardly be heard.

'Down!' the Canon repeated.

She flashed one terrible glance at Father Rassini, then

closed her eyes on the shame of it and wobbled to her knees on the carpet before her husband.

'Now,' the Canon said, 'now repeat after me: I beg forgiveness –'

It was as if she were stoppered for a few seconds and then the words, almost inaudible, faltered out: 'I beg forgiveness –'

'– for having interrupted the work of God –'

'– for having interrupted the work of God –'

'– and that of my husband –'

'– and that of my husband –'

'– who is His servant.'

'– who is –'

At this point Father Rassini, who was swallowing a revolting nausea, hauled himself up abruptly and blundered out of the room, down the clean hall, down the clean steps and into the rain.

'Oh, my God!' he kept mumbling to himself. 'Oh, my God my God my God!'

He pedalled slowly back to the highway and across town in the mouldering weather, the rain sputtering all over him, splashing, sluicing. The word 'horrible' kept forming in his mind. Horrible. Horrible. Somehow the quality of the rotted skies underscored – what was it? – goodness by antithesis, the virtue of the reasonable man. A kind of membrane tautened by his belief in the fabric of charity kept him dry.

He set the bike in the garage under the water-logged mango-trees. They were shifting their branches uneasily under the weight and in a sudden unshackled moment Father Rassini, who hadn't done such a boyish thing in years, turned his face up to them, opened his mouth and took communion. Unexpectedly he felt vigorous, alive. An inexplicable joy took hold of him as he gazed about the spongy garden, exotically beautiful with the dampened flames of hibiscus and poinsettia, limp now but still burning. Breathing deeply, he let out a sigh of – release? – of something, and turning from the unspeakable lustre of the leaves he mounted the back stairs to the kitchen.

Shriven, swimming in grace, he looked in and there, back to the door, hunched a little, frail, grey, his father sat shelling the peas.

Father Rassini watched him, watched him in shock.

Then abruptly he went back down the steps and walked out the gate.

3

Hunting the Wild Pineapple

3

After all, the house was nothing but an enormous barn, one gigantic living-room sixty by forty which was entered through the garage. Everything about the place groaned with bad taste.

Mr Pasmore ushered his guests – somehow his presence made us third person – from car to garage with the flair and pride of a talented lush, past rows of spigots labelled 'strawberries 7', 'pineapples 12', 'bananas 4'.

'It's simple,' he says twirling a pink gin, and he and his gin lean sideways with film-star lop-sided charm. 'But I'm so bloody lazy. Muscle-blood-bone-marrow-lazy.' His torpid eyes manage a practised twinkle. 'It's all mechanised now. Turn a knob and off race the nutrients. Saves a hell of a lot of trouble and the casuals do all the rough stuff. Weeding. Pine-grubs and so on. And I don't have to pause between drinks.'

He eases us into the living-room, which is split across one end by a twenty-foot curved tank of tropical fish, and twitches at a shoji screen. 'Bedrooms back there. Expand or contract a little according to taste. Makes the john a bit public, but then you can't have everything.'

Who has? But if I can horn in a bit on another's mummery . . .

I always seem to be explaining how I got where.

In a town like Mango social movements are amoebic – you'd better believe it, as they say in the US of A. I have dying memories of a middle-aged red-head on a bus to Florida: I want a meaningful relationship, she said. I mean I want to relate, she said. How do I get to express my total self? she asked. Baby, I say mentally, don't ask me, and dumped her in Jacksonville. Here there are these mercurial, spontaneous and apparently directionless surges to north and east; a lively fusion, a parting. The fusing can take eater and eaten by surprise: 'My *goo*'ness!' the little blonde had said in a bar somewhere off Madison, 'I didn't expect *this*!' It's not all carnal, I swear. Mere temporary interpretations, if you like, of what appears to be a strange new language which, despite the sameness of the semantic signals, is strange and new because the signals are given by a stranger. ('I've just changed guards!' Doc. Tripp commented bleakly after his third corrupt marriage.)

That's the fallibility of us. The new inflexion! Ah, *mamma mia*! A new meaning. This body, this face, these fingers, talk *diffrunt*! But they don't, of course; and reason asserts itself and the same dull old drone of the expected vision intrudes in those boardroom, bar-room, bedroom clichés I've heard, oh, I've heard, before.

I had moved, one translucent April, into a brief congruence that had originated as business and became shortly but intensely an ardent pattern of mutual succour. Mrs Crystal Bellamy, a calmly widowed South Georgian, impossibly researching the human geography of the north for a nonsense thesis, established a two months' base within the sticky filaments of my bed-and-breakfast web.

We passed swiftly from the manager-client nod to pleasant weather syllables to interrogatory clauses that contained all the primary fervour of two Vasco da Gamas colliding as they rounded the Horn. I'm interested in the violence of quick friendships. Snap up a pal! She was an articulate, golden-bunned lady with a certain piquancy of profile that was, at first encounter, blandly misleading. Be misled, I tell myself (and others, viciously), if only for the colour of expectancy. I am bearded now (arty or distinguished according to company), wooden-legged (the limp is captivating), and with a fringe of hang-ups, monstrous puritan-liberal growths like gall-wasp. No nodes on the skin, mark you: merely a flicker of epidermic sun-spotting – I call it bagassing – where the north has bitten me.

She wrestled me from Crusader Rabbit. My car became her car.

In a kind of tour-captain fever I distributed the country for her in hunks. We pursued lakes, craters, dams, limestone caves, ghost towns, abandoned mining camps, mission settlements, crocodile farms, hippie communes, sugar mills, prawn fleets, rich American marlin fishers, tin fossickers. We ranged north, south, west and, as far as weather would allow us, east. Her bun became sweetly loosened, my sun-spots increased, her note-book thickened. That's the how of it; and the specifics? Well, track them back to a well-intentioned buddy who wanted to prove we're not all grubbing away at the soil up here, that we're smooth, polished, and have swung quite nicely, ta ever so, into the sophisticated seventies.

So smooth that outside the house we are left gawking at a whopping heart-shaped swimming-pool filled with blue tears that blinked as a woman (his wife?) plunged from sight.

Mr Pasmore smiles at us.

'When Tubs emerges, if she does of course, she'll toss up some food. It's a pity in a way you didn't get here while there was more light. I could have shown you a bit more action. Muh-heen-while, I'll stiffen you a couple of stingers. You like that?'

We like that.

65

The sun took three drinks to go down. Mrs Bellamy gave an elegant paraphrase of academic purpose, and Tubs returned dripping from the pool and vanished behind a screen. Mr Pasmore did not seem to notice her.

'My, my!' he says, to Mrs Bellamy, 'we don't often get visitors of your calibre here.' Snapping the ice tongs. 'Another?'

We have another. Tubs emerges from the screen in a half-buttoned house-gown and heads straight for the bar where Mr Pasmore intercepts her with in-front-of-the-guests *bonhomie* and tells her she must meet these delightful people.

'Call me Crystal,' instructs Mrs Bellamy.

'Crystal,' Mrs Pasmore says obligingly and swigs a triple Scotch.

There are ice noises and Mr Pasmore puts heartbreak music on the tape-deck. Outside the world has gone black.

'What's for dinner, darling?' Mr Pasmore asks.

Tubs is a massive woman hewn from the one stone block. She stares vaguely at her handsome lug of a husband and momentarily her eyes cross with effort.

'There's a lobster somewhere.'

'Somewhere?'

'God knows.' She helps herself to another Scotch.

'Well, well,' Mr Pasmore says, smiling on us brightly, 'we'll just have to see if we can find it, won't we?'

The rummaging sounds from the screened-off kitchen section are terrible to hear. Tubs finishes off her drink and pours another.

'Crystal,' she says.

'Yes?' My bunned blonde registers polite guest stuff.

'Just musing,' Mrs Pasmore says.

We fight the conversation along for a bit, but it is only working two ways as our hostess sits with the lonely hootings of endless distances about her. From behind the screen it sounds as if a whole deep-freeze has been emptied onto the floor.

'My God!' Mr Pasmore cries flinging the screen to one side – and it's true: he's islanded on twenty square feet of frozen goodies. 'Got the damn thing! Afraid you'll have to wait a bit though. I need a drink after that.'

He comes back to us and bends spousily over his wife. 'I could kill you, my dear,' he says with frightful sweetness.

'Not now,' his wife says, regarding him for the first time. 'Not till after the guests go.'

'Certainly not till after the guests go,' Mr Pasmore says. Beside me Mrs Bellamy quivers with hunter's instinct.

Mr Pasmore is savaging the gin bottle. 'Fuel stop! Just the briefest of fuel stops and we'll do it together. Well, we three will. I think Tubs has opted out, haven't you, Tubs?'

'In,' Tubs says. 'I've opted in.'

There's nothing like doing things together my dad, my mum, my teachers all, all unblinkingly, blindly told me. Oh, my God, there's not! Eventually we got ourselves sorted out with lobster pieces and salad balanced on our laps. ('Tubs gets the small one! She didn't help one bit, did dear old Tubs!') The tape-deck changed its mood and Mr Pasmore sat as closely as possible to Mrs Bellamy and became highly technical as he thanked the good God for all growing things: which appeared to include her.

'Moonrise at nine. If you want,' he suggests, 'if you like, we'll go in search of the wild pineapple.'

'My!' Mrs Pasmore made her first conversational gambit in half an hour. Crystal smiled at me, him, even Tubs, uncertainly.

'Yes, oh yes! We'll do it by car' – he chucked ice into vodkas – 'and take a flash. Bring those. We'll need sustenance for the perils of the journey. Tubs won't come, will you, Tubs? She's rather had hunting the wild pineapple.'

67

But the moon was behind cloud as he backed his cumbersome elderly Ford from the garage and took it on full beam down the tracks to the paddocks. Our drinks slopped, but Mr Pasmore settled the car into low gear, steered with one arm curved affectionately round the wheel, and sipped elegantly. He was full of whimsy.

'No noise now,' he cautioned, disc-jockey style, as we bumped into the third plantation a mile from the house. 'Some of these big buggers might hear you. We'll go on foot from now on.'

Sitting in the swell of the noisy dark we finished our vodkas. Mr Pasmore's manly and chipper handsomeness should have reassured, but he was just sufficiently not quite like a well-known actor to appear not valid. The car was parked below a crest in the road with sea visible now on our right, its blanched acres distantly alive.

'You right, old man?' he inquires, doing the wrong thing as I stumble getting from the car. 'It's not much of a walk.' I hobble my answer. 'Just keep those flashes down, eh? I always like the element of surprise.' He lopes ahead with ball-toe bounce.

If I say that at this precise moment Mrs Bellamy unloosed her bun and the moon came out, you will charge me with the wretchedness of symbol. She did and it did and under the sudden blaze of both I barely noticed the whisper of her fingers on my arm. 'Don't worry,' she hummed with musical southern accent in my ear. 'He's what we call slightly off-centre.'

And why should I care? It's these half-way, middle-term, middling, mean hucksters who demean my spirit. I've always had a taste for the circumferential.

'He'll want you to douse that hair!' And the half-smile from under it.

We caught up with him at the bottom of the slope where he stood, finger-lipping a warning as we came up. He was doing cautionary peerings at the stickle-backed fields, a hunter's ear cocked to the grainy night. Suddenly he lunged sideways, football-tackle mode, and in the prancing beam of his flash his distorted shadow heaved and buckled at the base of the paddock-line. 'Lights!' he roared. 'Lights!' The paddock-line was racketing with movement. His body reeled and dived in the quaking air: a shambles of convulsed half-tone.

'Got you!' The voice was cracking at check-mate. 'Goh-hot you!'

'Oh, my God!' Mrs Bellamy whispers beside me, beginning to laugh, to laugh and run forward. His lank shape banked against moonlight. From his hand dangled a huge humped fruit.

Mrs Bellamy was catching on, astute Mrs Bellamy. 'Did it put up much fight?'

Mr Pasmore grinned and I am aware of teeth, the wet curve of lip.

'A flick of the wrist. A mere flick of the wrist,' he says, 'and it was all over. I am,' he says, 'in pretty fair condition. Here. It's for you.' On the word, he tattooed her arms with spikes; the head spears stabbed her chin. He lit, post-coitally I think nastily, a cigarette.

'Why, thank you!' Mrs Bellamy cries. 'You've given me the ears and the tail. But, my God, it's like a barb-wire melon!'

'Now, I like that,' Mr Pasmore murmurs. He turns down his flash and drops a pally arm on each of us. 'I like that very much. In fact, I like that like I like the two.'

'The two?' she asks. I don't. We are limping to the car. Yes. All of us. I'll transfer any disaffection, muddled as I am by hair and pineapples and the clear indifference of hot moonlight.

He's suave again, opening car doors with busy elegant flourishes.

'Two – um – two casuals. Two pickers. We do seem to get a funny crowd round here. Not, mark you, that I carp. No, no. I do not cuh-harp.' He lets in the clutch. 'In fact, it makes a break in a dull life. We have, you might have noticed, a very dull life. It's not often we get visitors like you. Style. Articulateness. The world, as it were, come to the pines.'

Despite the hair-flow Mrs Bellamy says rather tartly, 'You're making fun of us.'

'Mrs Bellamy – Crystal,' he says. 'As if. As very *if*. In a moment,' he adds catching my eye, 'I'll have to make love to this delightful lady simply to prove her wrong. Wrong wrong wrong. No seriously –' Oh, you're a no-but-seriously man, I think sourly. But he isn't. There's no 'but'. 'Nothing happens. That's our problem. Nothing happens.'

He went gloomy on us for half a mile.

'You wouldn't care, would you,' he asks as the house lights shoot between the trees, 'to take a little excursion? It will give Tubs time to achieve her coma. We can visit the – er – two.'

'More human geography,' I whisper. Mrs Bellamy's tanned fingers were rolling her hair into a sausage, but the profile was still bemusing.

He didn't wait for an answer but reversed the car suddenly with millimetric genius, swinging on rutty tracks to grind back between 'strawberries 1' and 'bananas 3' to an eastern fork. Another half mile – I am counting the death blows to my stump! – and a second house squatting on its moonlit hunkers, a half-veranda'd timber box watching through narrowed eyes like Jason's (there's culture for you!) the grey metal spikes of millions of pineapples.

Mr Pasmore drummed a neat riff on the wall beside the open front door, the over-familiar, paternalistic-presumptuous tat-a-tat, tat-tat, and emitted hearty cries of boss-lure down a passage blazing with unshaded electricity. Space goggled back at us. He rapped again and after another blazing empty minute a lardy perspiring Greek, a cliché of a Greek, hands clasped somewhere where his heart should be, waddled his smiles towards us. I thought he was smiling, I say now.

'Georgy,' Mr Pasmore asks, 'may we come in?' He was already in. 'I've brought you two delightful visitors. They have been exploring the possibility of the pineapple. Do you like that? The possibility of? I mean we all know the positivity of, don't we? What we want, oh, what we all so want want want is the possibility of? Georgy, do you believe in the possibility of the pineapple?'

Georgy giggled and the giggle made ripples on his flesh. So what else could the poor bastard do? He giggled and his eyes stayed dark as our names were offered and instantly forgotten. The introductions fluttered away like blank paper and came to rest in the mauve cube of a sitting-room which, too, was blazing like a bonfire of snappy magazine cut-outs tacked straight to the walls: glaciers, bad-lands, Alpine staccatos, palm-fringed nirvanas (they lie! – the motel complex has been chopped off by the fraudulent eye of the lens!) – all the clap-trap of plausible fable, while outside, outside, the grey lines of the armed fruit formed a desert of succulence.

There is a rhythm-bodied male of brunette intensity (even I can pick it!) shuffling cards by the window.

Mr Pasmore is saying with relish, 'And this is Tom. In fact, these are the tuh-who!'

Mr Pasmore can smile and smile and be, I am beginning to

think, somewhat of a shit; but the young man's smile matches up to his, and his height matches and his accent is what I call all haggis and kilt.

'It's a bonnie sound,' Mr Pasmore says with whimsy. 'I come here to practise m'Scots.' He practised it a bit. 'Y' no theenk ah bung eet on a beet?'

'Two what?' Tom asks, shuffling cards and smiling tensely. He is superbly good-looking and muscular and Georgy watches him with a moist and jealous eye.

'Two? Why, most interesting, most remarkable, most most. . . .' Voice-trail for hand-bafflement gestures. 'They are without a doubt' – turning to us – 'the best couple of workers I've had in years. Yes, years. So many, so many bums hit the coast this time of year and all they want to pick is the pay. But with Tom and Georgy, now, it's different. They've been with me – how long is it, Tam?'

'Three years.'

'Three. Well, thruh-hee is a long time. A long time in these parts. Most of them move on after one season and you never see them again. But Georgy and Tom, now, are part of the place. When the pines are finished they stay on for the replants. Georgy and Tom. They solace my evenings. They will even, if asked nicely, make us coffee. And, if asked really nicely, make music.'

'Are you asking nicely?' Tom inquires.

'Very. Oh, very.'

Indifferently, Tom fishes a mouth-organ from his pocket, teases us with an insolent jig during coffee noises. The coffee waddles back, Tom does bravura stuff to Mrs Bellamy's entranced delight, and Mr Pasmore, clasping hands round his mug and surveying the room, appears to be consuming us, not it. I always know when I'm being eaten, even the most delicate of nibbles. But do the others? Somehow being punched in the privacy, not the privates, gives such stunning pain I'm reduced even below whimper-level to shiver.

Tom shakes the saliva out of his mouth-organ, takes a gulp of coffee, and inspects Mrs Bellamy's quince and cream with rapid glances that our host easily nets.

She fills the void. Fatuously. 'Have you always done this?'

'Done what?'

'Well, casual work? Farming?'

'I don't know about thens. Only nows.'

Mr Pasmore is delighted.

'How about a song, Tom? He's a great ballad man, you know.'

And instantly, with an abruptness that was offensive, Tom launched into virile tenor that rang and roared across the room, out the open window and over the acres of pines. '"Och, Jock, where are y' trewsis?"' he sang, aggressively comic for six verses of *double entendre* hammered home with professional poise and eye-twinkles at each of us in turn: while Georgy poured more coffee and smiled possessively and watched enviously as Mrs Bellamy finally hooked the singer's eye for an entire verse.

The fat happiness of his possession is shaken.

'A good boy, eh? Good voice, eh?' Nodding and observing. Mr Pasmore is beating time with a playful spoon; but Tom drowns the taps with flourishes, to wind up with a smasher of a bow to the lady whose corruptibilty he is testing with mock hand on bogus heart.

'Oh yes oh yes! Only the most talented of puh-hickers!' Mr Pasmore cries. 'Only. I told you this is a show farm, my friends, my dear friends, and you are seeing the *spécialité de la muh-haison!*'

'You're surely quite an artist,' Mrs Bellamy says, reluctant to release that hand on the heart. At least she's got his eyes! 'I suppose you've done a bit of singing professionally, have you?'

'A wee bit. Here and there.'

'Oh, it was so good! Very, very good. Could we beg another?'

She's fusing. Relating. She's on the Florida bus. She's giving him the Martini eye in a singles bar. Her orbs glut on his hip-moves as he swings into a chair and rides it back to front.

'I. . . .' Georgy appeared to be gulping. 'I . . . I. . . .' His sausage fingers are plucking at her arm. 'I, too.'

I've seen it. You've seen it. We've seen it. Want me to conjugate all the forms of envy? It's rather nice, this, turning into a cipher recorder in the middle years, slapping my wooden-leg for comfort while I note – note, mark you – the gobbledy-gook of sad little human rivalries setting flesh aquake. Oh, I'm sad for them all right. Sad sad sad.

Crystal (the moment calls for intimacy) releases her eyes unwillingly to turn and stare, not resentfully – interestedly, at the fingers on her arm.

'I, too,' Georgy repeats.

'You sing?'

'No, no. An artist. I am an artist.' His eyes are on Tom with love and loathing. 'I paint. I am an artist.'

'An artist?'

Georgy nods and beams.

'Aye, he is that,' Tom agrees. I am the only one to catch the wink. 'Gie us a wee glance at same, Georgy.'

Mr Pasmore, raree-show proprietor, becomes golden with pride. 'Come on, Georgy. Bruh-hing out those etchings, those fabled canvases. If you won't come and see mine,' he adds in a whisper to Mrs Bellamy. 'Eh?'

Georgy's eagerness, all gulps and agreement and smirks of

tumid promise, is frightful. Bloated and puffy with his moment, he waddles off to the bedroom and we nurse our discomfort – I nurse mine; Mr Pasmore is asimmer with something – until he limps back with a shabby grocery carton that he heaves onto the table.

'There!' he says. And beams.

We wait.

He smiles before his backdrop of deadly cut-outs, centre-stage at last, clutching his moment.

'Go on, Georgy,' Mr Pasmore says lightly. 'Open up!'

Georgy folded back the cardboard flaps, did an all-thumbs fumble at a protective layer of brown paper, and scooped out half a dozen sketches that he spread on the table before us as if he were fanning a royal flush.

Spanking girls they were, big-thighed, vilely luscious cartoons of comic-strip emptiness, copies of an archetype sex goddess that came with the first fifty lessons. Kid-stuff. Clumsy. Crude.

What to say?'

'Why, Georgy,' Mrs Bellamy says, not daring to look at his eager and waiting face, 'they're really good. Really.' She doesn't look at anyone but keeps shifting her fingers' desperate interest from one sketch to the next, a shade too enthusiastic. 'I'd really love to have one. May I?'

Does Georgy's delighted vanity then do to the others what it's doing to me? Does it?

He puts the sketches aside and purses his mouth critically.

'But that is before,' he says, 'before I am enrolled. These I have sent them. They are trials, you understand.' He is engrossed with explanation. 'To see if I can be an artist perhaps. And they take me, you know. They take me.' He can hardly contain his joy. 'Oh, very expensive. A lot of money. But you send away, you see, and they send you . . .

there are fifty lessons. They say I have. . . .' He can't find the
word and sausage hands wave helplessly.

'Promise, Georgy,' Tom says, helping him. 'They say you
have promise. Lots o' promise.'

'That's it. That is what I have. Promise.'

He sucks the word with his head on one side. 'I am enrolled
since two years now.'

He dives into the carton again, his pudgy arms milling
around, and drags out another box. The two unused brushes
lie beautifully beside unsqueezed tubes, three rows of them.
The palette is unstained. Georgy runs his fingers lovingly
over it.

'Fifty lessons.'

Below the paint-box is a great stack of gleaming knot
paper. Reverently Georgy lifts the paper block out and places
it carefully, gently, and perfectly square beside his other
things. His fingertips keep stroking the paper.

'And all this,' he says. 'I am an artist.'

We all looked at the untouched, well-loved objects.

'How's about more coffee, Thomas?' Mr Pasmore asks.
'Or prithee a Scotch?'

But Georgy it is who hauls himself up. 'I,' he says, 'I make
you more coffee. I make you beautiful coffee this time.' He is
radiant with possession.

'And when are you sending in that first lesson, Georgy?'
Mr Pasmore asks spitefully. 'When are you sending in the
fuh-hirst, eh?'

I see Tom flash at him and catch the hate before the laugh.

But Georgy turns back to us from the kitchen door and he
is still doped with the dream, wagging, smiling benignly,
benignly, at the lunatic acres beyond the open window.

'Soon,' he says. 'Soon now.'

4

A Northern Belle

4

The night Willy Fourcorners sat with me, awkward in his Christian clothing, he told me, between the clubbing blocks of rain, what it was like sometimes to be black in these parts. He's sat with me other nights as well and what he told me of this one or that, this place or that, was like taking a view from the wrong side of the fence. Wrong's not the word. Photographing in shadow, the object that is? No. I'm still hunting the wild simile. It was . . . it was like inspecting the negative, framing and hanging its reversals, standing back to admire, then crying in despair, 'But it's all different!'

People I knew, he knew, but he knew them some other-how – as if he saw Lawyer Galipo and Father Rassini from the lee side of the banks of heaven. I asked him once why he'd ever left his little house on the outskirts of Tobaccotown, and he was silent a long time. I coddled his silence and at last he told me. I put his story onto their stories and still I get one story.

This is Willy's story, my words.

She was born in one of those exhausted, fleetingly timbered places that sprang up round the tin mines of the north. Not in the poverty of a digger's shack, let it be understood, but in the more impressive veranda'd sprawl of one of those cedar houses that loiter in heavy country gardens. How capture the flavour of those years? Horse-rumps, sweat, hard liquor, crippled shanties, all forgotten in the spacious hours after lunch and before tea when baking fragrance settled as gently as the shadows across and into the passion-vined trellis.

A porky child with a fine cap of almost white dead-straight hair, her body gave no indication of the handsome bones that were to emerge in late adolescence. Skip some years. Now we have her at fourteen bounding confidently across the town hard-court, shimmering with sweat, her hair longer now, darkening now, still fine and unmanageable; but it's still no pointer to the strong-minded Clarice of nineteen who, despite a profile of pleasing symmetry, still boyishly racquet-scooped balls, served low and hard, and later dispensed lemon squash in the tin side-line shed where other acceptables of the town gathered each Saturday afternoon.

She had early the confidence of her class. Her father was a mine manager and owner. 'AG' they called him, and he knew to a nicety what line of familiarity to draw with the blacks who still hung about the perimeters of town, even instigating a curfew for them, but was less certain when it came to men of his own colour. Which was either bright red or mottled white. In snapshots from the period he, heavily moustached and mutton-chopped beside his wife, dominated rows of sawney after-picnic guests. She always appeared formidably silked and hatted and her bust was frightening. 'Breasts' is somehow too pretty, too delicate a word to describe that shelf of righteousness on which many a local upstart had foundered. Along with the bust was a conde-scending familiarity with the town's priest, two ministers of other religions, and four members of parliament whom she had seen come and helped go. Clarice was an only child, not as much of a son as the father had hoped for and something less of a daughter; but with the years her looks fined and softened; and if she was not in fact a beauty privilege made her just as desirable in a country where a fine bank account is as good for launching a thousand ships as a face: it's even better.

Her mother was determined Clarice would marry well, but no one was ever quite well enough.

Motor-cars and Clarice's teens created small tensions. There were various young men; but the town had little to offer beyond bank- and railway-clerks, or the sons of Italian tobacco farmers whose morals the mother suspected to be doubtful. Should too long a time elapse between the drawing-up of a young man's car and Clarice's flushed entry to the house, her mother would tighten her mouth, draw up that juridical bust, and struggle to find words that were at once proper and admonitory. She was rarely able to draw that nice balance and one afternoon, as she worked with her daughter in the kitchen crumbing butter and flour for scones, she said without preamble and quite formally:

'I was once attacked by a sexually maddened blackfellow.'

Clarice was startled.

'That is why.' Her mother shut her lips tightly and a little line was ruled.

'Why what?'

'Why you must keep men – all men – at a distance.'

'All men?' inquired Clarice. 'Or just sexually maddened blackfellows?'

'You are too young, Clarice,' her mother said sharply, 'to use such words. Girls of sixteen should not even know such words.'

'But I don't understand,' Clarice persisted. 'Were you –?' she hesitated. 'Harmed' seemed not an exact enough word. 'Were you carnally known?'

Her mother fainted.

'I do not know where,' she later gabbled to Clarice's father, 'where this – this child – could pick up such . . . I have done all . . . appalling knowledge . . . how the good nuns . . . wherever . . . she must be protected from. . . .'

She spoke at length to her daughter on the necessity of virtue, the rigours of beauty, of chastity, the clean mind, and the need to expunge lust. She went so far as to summon Father Rassini to give spiritual advice. She read her daughter an improving poem. Clarice listened to all this with an expression on her face as if she were trying to remember a knitting pattern. Young men were discouraged from calling. Her current bank-clerk went away in the army and Clarice, after dreadful scenes in which she finally proved herself her father's daughter, took the little branch train to the coast, caught the main line south, and burrowed into essential war industry.

The city was only partly strange to her, for she had been educated at a southern convent where her only achievements had been to stagger the nuns by the ferocity with which she played badminton and Mendelssohn's *Rondo Capriccioso*. She revealed no other talents. They taught her a little refined typing and book-keeping, insufficient to addle or misdirect any feminine drives; enough French to cope with a wine list in the better restaurants; and some basic techniques in water-colours. She had a full and vigorous voice that dominated, off-key, the contralto section of the school choir for three years, but even this mellowed into suitable nuances before the onslaught of the mistress in charge of boarders.

'My dear Clarice,' she would reprove icily, 'you are not a man.'

'*Non, ma mère*,' Clarice would reply dutifully, giving the little curtsey this particular order required.

'And further, you seem to forget that men do not. . . .oh,

never mind!' Mother Sulpice rolled her fine brown eyes upwards, a kind of ecstatic St Teresa, and swished off with her beads rattling.

The boarders pondered Mother Sulpice.

'You can see she was quite beautiful,' Clarice's best friend, a thumping girl, commented doubtfully. 'Quite Renaissance.'

'Do you think she was jilted in love?' The students spent much time in these speculations.

'Oh, I heard. I heard.'

'What? What did you hear?'

'I shouldn't say.'

'Oh, come on! What?'

'My mother told me something.'

'Told you what?'

'I shouldn't really say.'

'Oh, yes you should,' Clarice insisted. She kicked quite savagely at the iron railing of the terrace that looked out over Brisbane hills. 'By not telling me you are creating an occasion of sin.'

Thumper went pink. 'I'm not. How could I be?'

'Who knows what I shall think,' Clarice said cunningly. 'I could think almost anything. In fact, I do think almost anything.'

She looked slyly at her friend and observed the moral contortion with interest.

'You've got to promise,' Thumper said, 'that you won't tell.'

'Well?'

'Do you promise?'

'Of course.'

'Well,' Thumper said with a pretty play of hesitancy, 'well, she was engaged. Before she entered.'

'And what then?'

'He died. He was killed in France. It wasn't,' she said, lowering her voice in horror, 'a true vocation.'

'Oh, stuff that,' Clarice said. 'How did it happen?'

'Mummy said it was quite tragic.' Clarice saw her friend's eyes grow moist and noticed she was getting a new pimple. 'He was running to regain the trenches and he ran the wrong way. He was dreadfully short-sighted.'

Clarice wanted to laugh. Instead, she looked at her friend hard and asked, 'Do you think they'd had sexual intercourse?'

'Now you *will* have to go to confession!' her friend said.

'Poor Mother Sulpice!' Clarice sighed.

But it was for her, perhaps for the wrong reasons, transfiguration.

She studied the nun's graceful walk, imitated the Isadora-like arabesques of her hands, modulated her voice, and began training her hair into expressive curves across her ears.

'How Clarice has changed!' the nuns observed with relief. 'She's growing up at last.'

In class, her mind closed to the finer points of the redundant *ne*, she sought for and thought she discovered the delicate prints of tragedy on Mother Sulpice's completely calm face.

'That will be the way I will bear it,' she said to herself.

After she left home the first job she obtained was as an office assistant in a factory supplying camouflage tents to the troops. She left the day the senior accountant, who was married, suggested they take in dinner and a show. When she leapt offendedly onto a tram, an American serviceman asked could he help her with her bag. She had no bag but was so confused by the nature of his offer that before she had gone three blocks she found herself in conversation with him. He told her many lies, but those she most vividly remembered were about a cotton plantation in Georgia, an interrupted semester at Yale, and no engagement of the heart, legal or otherwise. As she dressed in her YWCA cubicle for her third outing with him, she kept telling herself it was Mother Sulpice all over again, and she dropped her firm tanned neck, glanced back into the speckly mirror, and lowered her eyes in unconscious but perfect parody.

On the sixth outing seven days after they had met, he attempted to take her to bed, but she resisted with much charm. On the seventh he told her he had been drafted to the Pacific and they then exchanged deeply emotional letters that she read again and again, all the time thanking God for the good training which had prevented 'that' from happening. 'That' was happening all about her. Thumper was pregnant to a marine who had crossed the horizon without leaving any other memento of his visit. Men were all like that, Thumper assured Clarice between her sobs. Clarice thought it a pity her nose got so red when she cried.

Clarice managed to repress her feelings of righteousness and exultation that she was the one spared, and after she had seen her friend take a sad train back to her stunned parents up country she slid into Thumper's job in an army canteen. She was totally unprepared for a letter some months later from Roy telling her he had married a nurse in Guam because he had to. 'Honey,' he wrote, 'you will always be very special to me. You will always be my one true love, the purest I have ever known.' He was lying again, but she was spared the knowledge of this.

She was not built for pathos. The troubles of others found in her a grotesque response of incomprehension. She kept meeting more and more men, but they all failed to please, were not rich enough or wise enough or poor enough if wise, or were too worldly or unworldly. And through all of this, growing steadily older and handsomer, she bore her singleness like an outrageous pledge of success.

At parties when other girls more nervous than she spilt

claret cup or trifle on the hostess's carpet at those endless bring-a-plate kitchen teas she seemed always to be attending, she would say offhandedly, 'Don't worry. It's not *her* trifle,' and go on flirting tangentially and unconsummatedly with this or that. She was moving up the ranks and knew a lot of colonels now.

When the war was over she settled more or less permanently into a cashier's desk at a large hotel where for half a dozen years she was still courted by desperate interstate commercial travellers who, seeing her framed between the stiff geometry of gladioli, found a *quattrocento* (it was the hair-style) mystique which they did not recognise as such but longed to explore. She accepted their pre-dinner sherries with every symptom of well-bred pleasure, went to films, dog-races, and car-trials with them, but always bade them firm good-nights outside her own apartment.

Then her hair began to show its first grey.

Her father died suddenly shouting at a foreman; and after Clarice had gone home to help out her mother held onto her for quite a while, determined to see her daughter settled. Rallying from grief, she arranged picnics, dances, barbecues, musical evenings, card suppers; yet even she gave up when Clarice returned home far too early from a picnic race-meeting with a *fin de siècle* languor about the eyes.

'Where's that nice Dick Shepworth?' her mother demanded from a veranda spy-post.

'At the races, I suppose.'

'You left him there?'

'Yes. He is suffering from encroaching youth.'

'But, my God!' cried her mother. 'He's the manager of two cane mills with an interest in a third.'

'He holds his knife badly,' Clarice said, picking up a malformed piece of knitting.

'You must be mad,' her mother said.

'And he chews with his mouth open.'

'Oh, my God!'

She was dead by the end of the party season. Clarice got Father Rassini to bury her alongside AG, sub-divided the property, sold at a profit and, having invested with comfortable wisdom in an American mining corporation, retired into her parents' house and spent her days in steady gardening. It became a show place. It was as if all her restrained fertility poured out into the welter of trees and shrubs; and if the rare and heady perfumes of some of them made occasional sensual onslaughts she refused to acknowledge them.

The day she turned forty she bought herself a dog.

He was a fine labrador who established his rights at once, learnt smartly to keep away from the seedling beds and to share her baked dinner. They ate together on the long veranda which stared down at the mined-out hills beyond the garden, and the tender antithesis of this transferred the deepest of green shadows into her mind, so that she found herself more and more frequently talking to Bixer as if he had just made some comment that deserved her reply. Her dependence on him became engrafted in her days: he killed several snakes for her, barked at the right people, and slept, twitching sympathetically with her insomnia, by the side of her bed. She only had to reach down to pat Roy, a colonel, a traveller, or even Dick Shepworth, and they would respond with a wag of the tail.

Although so many years had passed since her parents' deaths, Clarice still believed she had a position in the town and consequently gave a couple of duty dinner parties each year – but not willingly – to which she invited old school friends, townsfolk who still remembered her father, and occasionally Father Rassini. He dreaded the summons, for she was a bad cook; but attended, always hopeful of some generous donation. Aware of this, she would keep him sweating on her Christmas contribution till it was almost Easter; and when she finally handed him the envelope they both remembered her stoniness as he had talked to her, thirty years ago now, about the sins of the flesh. He'd been young, too; and whenever he sat down to an especially lavish meal at some wealthy parishioner's home he recalled her cool look as she had asked, 'Are you ever tempted, Father?'

As her muscles shrank the garden acre flexed its own, strengthened and grew more robust than a lover. There were rheumatic twinges that worried her. One day when she went to rise from where she had been weeding a splendid planting of dwarf poinsettia, the pain in her back was so violent she lay on the grass panting. Bixer nosed around, worried and whimpering, and she told him it was nothing at all; but she thought it was time she got a little help.

She was fifty when she took in Willy Fourcorners as gardener. He was an elderly Aborigine, very quiet, very gentle, who had been for a long time a lay preacher with one of the churches. Clarice didn't know which one, but she felt this made him respectable. Willy wore a dark suit on Sundays, even in summer, and a tie. He would trudge back from the station sometimes, lugging a battered suitcase and, passing Clarice's house and seeing her wrenching at an overgrowth of acalypha, would raise his stained grey hat and smile. The gesture convinced Clarice that though he was a lesser species he was worthy, and she would permit herself to smile back, but briefly.

'Willy,' she said one day, emerging from the croton hedge, 'Willy, I wonder could I ask your help?'

Willy set down his bag in the dust and rubbed his yellow-palmed hands together.

'Yeah, Miss Geary. What's the trouble then?'

She came straight to the point.

'I need help with the garden, Willy.' She was still used to command and the words came out as less of a request than she intended. She was devastated by the ochreous quality of his skin so close to hers and a kindliness in the old eyes she refused to admit, for she could not believe in a Christian blackskin, preacher or not. 'It's all getting too much for me.'

Willy's face remained polite, concerned but doubtful. He was getting on himself and still worked as a handyman at the hardware store. On week-ends he preached.

'Only got Saturdays,' he said.

'Well, what's wrong with Saturday?'

'I like to keep it for m'self.'

Clarice struggled with outrage.

'But wouldn't you like a little extra money, Willy?'

'Not that little, Miss Geary,' Willy said.

Clarice's irritation riveted at once upon the simple smiling face, and unexpectedly, contrarily, she was delighted with his show of strength.

'I'm a fair woman,' she said. 'You'd get regular wages. What I'd give anyone.'

Willy nodded. He still smiled through the sweat that was running down his face, down his old brown neck and into the elderly serge of his only suit.

'Please,' Clarice heard herself pleading. 'Just occasionally. It would be such a help, Willy. You see, I can't handle the mowing these days.' And she produced for him what she had managed to conceal from almost everyone, a right hand swollen and knobbed with arthritis, the fingers craned painfully away from the thumb into the beginnings of a claw.

Willy looked at her hand steadily and then put out one finger very gently as if he were going to touch it. She tried not to wince.

'That hurts bad, eh?' he said. 'Real bad. I'll pray for you, Miss Geary.'

'Don't pray for me, Willy,' Clarice said impatiently. 'Just mow.'

He grinned at that and looked past her at the thick mat of grass that was starting a choking drive about the base of the trees.

'Saturday,' he said. 'Okay.'

He came every few weeks after that and she paid him well; and after a year, as her right hand became worse and the left developed symptoms, he began to take over other jobs – pruning, weeding, planting out, slapping a coat of paint, fixing a rotted veranda board. She grew to look forward to the clear Saturday mornings when with Bixer, ancient, dilapidated, sniffing behind her, she directed him down side paths as he trimmed and lopped the flashy outbursts of the shrubs. Although at first she tended to treat him and pay him off as she would imagine AG to have done, gradually she became, through her own solitariness, aware of him as a human; so that after a time, instead of returning to the veranda for her cup of tea after taking him his, she got into the habit of joining him at the small table in the side garden.

'Where is it you get to, Willy,' she asked one Saturday morning as they drank their tea, 'when you take the train down to the coast?'

'Don't go to the coast, Miss Geary.'

'Where do you go then?'

'Jus' down as far as Mango.'

'Mango?' Clarice exclaimed. 'Why would you want to go to Mango?'

'Visit m'folks there,' he said. 'Got a sister there. Visit her kids. She got seven.'

'Seven,' Clarice murmured. 'Seven.' She thought of Thumper. 'That's a large number, I must say.'

'They're good kids,' Willy said. 'My sister, see, she'd like me to go an' live down there now they're gettin' on a bit.'

'She's younger than you, then, Willy?'

'Yeah. Fair bit younger.'

'And have you any, Willy? Any children, I mean?' She knew he lived alone, had done since she had come back to live.

'Two,' he said. 'Two boys. Wife died of the second one. But they been gone a long time now. Real long time.'

'Where to?'

'South,' he said. 'Down south.'

'And what do they do? Do they write?'

'Yeah. Come home sometimes an' stay with m'sister. One's a driver for some big factory place. Drives a truck, see? Other feller, he's in the church. He's trainin' to go teachin' one of them mission places.'

'Well, he's certainly done well,' Clarice said. 'You must be very proud of him.'

'Pretty proud,' old Willy said. 'Teachin' up the mission when he's through. Up Bamaga way he'll be. Might get to see him then, eh?'

'Do you get lonely, Willy?' she asked. But he didn't answer.

Bixer developed a growth. When Clarice noticed the swelling in his belly she summoned the vet from Finecut who took one look and said, 'I'll give him a shot if you like.'

'Get out!' Clarice said.

She cared for him as far as she was able, but he could only shamble from bedroom to veranda where he'd lie listless most of the day in the hot northern sun, not even bothering to snap at the flies. He lost control of his bladder and whimpered the first time he disgraced himself on the bedroom floor. Clarice whimpered herself as she mopped up.

Willy found her crying over the dog one Saturday morning. Bixer could hardly move now, but his eyes looked their recognition as Willy bent over him.

'Best you get him put away, Miss Geary,' Willy advised, touching the dog with his gentle fingers. 'Pretty old feller now.'

'Help me, Willy,' she said. 'I can't do that.'

He brought along an old tin of ointment he'd used for eczema on a dog of his own, and though he knew it wouldn't help he rubbed it in carefully, if only to help her.

'There y'are, Miss Geary,' he said looking up from where he knelt by the panting dog. 'That might do the trick.'

She was still tearful but she managed a smile at him.

'Thank you, Willy. You're a good man.'

It didn't do the trick; and when finally on one of the endless bland mornings of that week she found he had dragged away to die under the back garden bushes she could hardly bear it. She sat for a little on the veranda, which became populous with the ghosts of the endless summer parties of her youth. The smack of tennis balls came from a hard-court. The blurred voices of bank-clerks and railway-clerks and service men and travellers, and even the sound of Dick Shepworth eating, hummed and babbled along the empty spaces where her mother still sat in her righteous silks.

She put on her sun-hat and walked down town to the hardware store, where she found Willy sweeping out the yard.

'You've got to come, Willy,' she said. 'He's dead.'

'Strewth, Miss Geary. I'm real sorry. Real sorry.'

'You'll have to help me bury him, Willy. I can't dig the hole.'

'Strewth, Miss Geary,' Willy said. 'Don' know whether I kin leave.'

He propped himself on his broom handle and regarded her awkwardly. She was trying hard not to cry. He felt all his age, too, leaning there in the hot sun thinking about death.

'I'll fix that,' she said. She was still AG's daughter.

After it was over she made some tea and took it out to the garden. Willy looked hopelessly at her with his older wisdom.

'Don't you worry none, Miss Geary,' he kept saying. 'I'll get you a new little pup. A new one. Me sister, she got plenty. Jus' don' worry, eh?'

But she was sobbing aloud now, frightful gulping sounds coming from her as she laid her head on her arms along the table.

'Please, Miss Geary,' Willy said. 'Please.'

He touched her hand with his worn one, just a flicker, but she did not notice, did not look up, and he rubbed his hand helplessly across his forehead.

'Look,' he said, 'I got to be goin' soon. But true, me sister she's got these two dogs an' they jus' had pups. I'll get you one of theirs, eh? You'd like that. There's this little brown feller, see, with a white patch. He's a great little dog. You'd like that, eh?'

Slowly she lifted her head, her face ruined with weeping, and saw the old black man and the concern scribbled all over his face.

'Oh, Willy,' she said, 'that's so kind of you. It really is. But it won't make any difference.'

'But it will,' Willy argued, human to human. 'Nex' time I come to mow I'll bring him back. You see. You'll love him.'

He pushed his chair back, came round the table and stood beside her, wanting to cry himself a bit, she looked that old an' lost. She looked up at him, messy with grief, and Willy put his old arm round her shoulders and gave her a consoling pat.

'There,' he said. 'Don' you mind none.'

He'd never seen a face distort so.

She began to scream and scream.

5

Petals from Blown Roses...

5

Down by the bar at the end of the pool Ella Fitzgerald was telling them to take love easy easy easy and the women with skin like bark kept taking the conversation easy with two gate-crashers from a lugger. No one quite knew how they got there and by this stage no one cared. By eleven the group had re-disposed itself under the chuk-chuk of the hi-fi whose avant-garde globular speakers dangled amid the fern baskets and allamanda vines like magenta carbuncles.

This is another house along the coast. And other people. And the same house and the same people. One party is all parties. Why bother? Why exist? There is only one *gaucho*, as Borges says.

The drink and the heartiness and the heat are taking them in and out of the water like yo-yos; and after a while, after a very little while, the younger women are flinging tops aside in a kind of brazen flat-chestedness and offering themselves to the gloze of half-light and aquamarine.

I watch Mrs Waterman sitting serenely in a corner perhaps expecting a parallel gesture or diagonal revelation from the men. It does not come. But in a flash I'm there at the Nature Club, in memory only, I assure you, where in pseudo-metaphysical release members pingpong, hurdle, ball-net, divested of all civilisation's rags. In the club's wet tropic air, lotioned against March flies and mosquitoes, behind languid banks of jungle that shelter their philosophic inquiries, they had seemed vigorously mad, especially at tea-breaks when the sudden clutching of glasses of carrot juice stressed their nakedness. Oh, the strategy of plates!

'What can I get you?' Bosie Hackendorf asked, coming naked from the poolside. She was a stubby blonde with almost no breasts and her nipples appeared quite startled by this.

'A double gin,' Mrs Waterman said firmly.

'Ice?'

'Please.'

'Tonic?'

'Not even the suggestion of it.'

She was one of those women I always expect to hear say dreamily 'how sweet the moonlight sleeps upon the Chase Manhattan Bank'. They can be seen at openings: tapestries, paintings, ethnic wood carvings, even tarted up displays of pioneer cooking utensils (she was the first woman in Reeftown to get a bed with brass balls): their calm appraising eye and smile indicate that they understand nothing but embrace the lot. Mrs Waterman's cheque book was always poised to trap the *objet juste*. Its pages would obligingly flutter open and some enraptured dead-beat who had only lately begun to understand the prestige racketeering that now accompanied what roughneck peasants had crafted infinitely better centuries before would alight, as it were, on the blank paper and coax the ball-point of her patronage.

She sits now ignoring her hostess's startled nipples. They ruffled her sense of orderliness, but she keeps a benign and smiling eye upon the pool where the host, a trifle old for it but determinedly boyish, is pummelling hell out of a shiny black rubber raft.

Bosie follows her gaze.

'I do wish,' she says thoughtfully and with dreadfully careful vowels, 'that Brain would speak nicely. I do like a man to speak nicely.' Pensively she rubs the rim of Mrs Waterman's glass under one nipple.

'He seems,' Mrs Waterman says, flinching, 'perfectly adequate to me.'

'Oh, no. Really. No. No no no no. He will keep saying things like "beaut" and "lousy" – you know, like those terrible telly ads for the terribly normal man. He really is dreadfully careless. The children,' she accuses, looking hard into Mrs Waterman's eyes and then mine, 'the children – and thank goodness Bims and Chaps are away at boarding-school – tend to be influenced. I simply don't want that. I don't ever want that. It's so important for them to speak nicely.'

'Why?' Mrs Waterman asks brutally. Her eyes are riveted on her drink glass.

'My dear! Their friends! The people they'll meet!'

'And see,' Mrs Waterman adds. 'Very much "and see". All, all makes its mark.'

Mr Waterman, who rarely attended parties, wrote the cryptic crosswords for half a dozen papers and magazines. The results of living with his preoccupation had given him irregular attitudes to the more banal objects of life. It was impossible for him to glimpse some autumnal grove of tamarisks without his mentally tabulating 'a grateful expression mother hazards among shrubs'. Or coming upon some possibility nugget in his steady perusal of mythological material ('Wonderful source, my dear! Wonderful source!'), he would classify unicorns as 'varsity problems referable to chiropodists and other fantastic creatures'. This had its slow, its steady, its heavily rhythmic effect upon Mrs Waterman, who attended more and more church hoy drives, opened fêtes, launched yachts, slapped token mortar on foundation stones, cut ribbons and, where politically possible, jerked hydro-electric levers.

Mr Waterman was, also, a foundation member of the metric society. He was the first in the district to think in millimetres of rain, kilometres of road, kilograms of body fat and the metric statistics of wanted criminals. When he and Mrs Waterman did their biennial culture junket to Europe, he took enormous pleasure in supplying details for his passport. 'One point eight five four three metres,' he wrote against 'height'; 'eyes' – 'blue'. He would chide his wife mildly. 'No, dear. No, no. You are one point six four one two metres.' Against 'colour of eyes' she wrote 'glazed'.

She says now to Bosie, 'I like men to *think* nicely.' Her italics remain proper. 'You haven't forgotten my drink, have you?'

She kept remembering something he had said last night.

'It's possible, my dear, really possible to reduce time to units of ten. Let's take the decade, say. That means this year, 1976, one thousand nine hundred and seventy-six years after the birth of our saviour, could be expressed as AD 19.76.'

'I thought Christ was born in 5 BC.'

He ignored her.

'Now if we take the decade' – he was really warming to it – 'as embracing the span of one hundred and twenty months, then it should be possible to gather not only the month of the year but – let's see. . . .' He began mumbling and scribbling a great deal. 'Yes – even the day of the week as a fraction of seven times four eighty. So let's see – if we continue to regard Sunday as the first day of the week, then Thursday, say, would be . . . no, wait a minute. Let's take the *days* per month. That's it! The *days*.' His whole face was illuminated. '*So.* The third Thursday in this March would be the twenty-seventh part of thirty-one of the third of one hundred and twenty. Or . . . to put it more simply –'

Mrs Waterman had left the room.

'I mean think *simply*,' she adds as Bosie turns away. 'One might even say – normally.'

'Oh there's nothing queer about Brain.' (He spells it Brian.) 'Nothing at all. He's so – so normal. Coarsely normal, you might say.'

'You might indeed.'

'Really!' Bosie's face goes blunt. 'I'll get your gin.'

'Oh, my dear,' Mrs Waterman assures her, 'of course I meant nothing like that!'

Yoicking and cat-calls rocket from the pool. 'Hey, c'mon in! *C'mon!* In! In!' There are guggle sounds.

I fetch my own drink and on the way back to our shadowy corner dole out an absolutionary sprinkle to two boyish girl nudes who pluck at me.

'All these bodies! These bodies!' Mrs Waterman is sipping once more.

'Uh-huh!' I agree. Listless. 'But why don't we get some *women* in to liven things up?'

Mrs Waterman is a yummy forty-five. Her cool and beautiful face gazes appraisingly at me from beneath a dense simplicity of dark hair and she smiles with a terrible slowness, her ladylike fingers delicately holding her gin glass like a question mark.

Beyond the pool, feverish under light, the saffron curtain of guinea vine dangled banners of enormous and dynamic promise. Gorgeous flowers swung – rollicked would be a better word – between trees, and if there were a slightly unpleasant stench from their pannicles no one seemed to notice. The gin helped, too, Mrs Waterman appeared to be finding, as she watched flowers and her more personally quiet manias swing in space with the blossom.

'Do you swim?'

'Only to frighten people.' I patted my bogus leg.

She laughed vigorously somewhere below middle C. Bosie was back again, hovering on our edges; but Mrs Waterman raised her glass, drank deeply this time and laughed again.

'And *do* you?'

'Only the weak-minded.'

'Then come on in.'

The pool was a fury of horse-play. Chlorinated water sloshed about our feet with spilt beer. The hi-fi belted into the night.

'*C'mon!*' a voice woofed from the raft. 'Get y'gear off!'

'There. You see what I mean,' Bosie whimpered, pained. 'You do see what I mean about Brain?'

Mrs Waterman seemed to be tracking the spoor of some unsolved problem. Her eyes fixed thoughtfully on the rocking surface of the pool while one manicured hand patted my arm absently.

'I think,' she stated judgmentally, 'that I will.'

Without speed, with a kind of deft but leisurely sacrificial motion, Mrs Waterman got her gear off.

Deliberately she stepped forward into the pool-side light, her body impressively sumptuous and white. For a full minute she stood smiling abstractedly while the guests goggled and the hi-fi blared solo, then she dived, to emerge near the raft on which her host lay sprawled with two of the girls. When she turned I saw she was smiling her fête-opener's smile at them.

Something seemed to have clamped our host's tongue as she pulled herself neatly onto the raft beside him where, propped Récamier on one elbow, she contemplated the stilled waters.

'Delicious!' she commented. We could hear her at the edge. 'It really is absolutely delicious in.'

Her host was staring at her as if he'd been whacked.

'God!' he said. 'God! You're all right!'

Mrs Waterman smiled. 'There's really nothing like getting rid of the trappings, is there?' she asked and ran her hands over a frightful silkiness of skin.

Brain kept dragging soaked hair back off his forehead nervously. Admiration reduced him to stammer.

'It's your cool! Your bloody cool! Your . . . .' He fought around for it for a bit. 'Your elegance.'

'Thank you,' Mrs Waterman said simply.

Her host kept staring.

'In fact,' he said loudly, to our fascination, 'you're the only one here with any tits at all.'

'Oh, my God, Brain,' his wife cried, 'there you go again!'

'Not at all,' Mrs Waterman replied, disclaiming all credit with a modesty that was marvellous to see. 'Oh, truly, not at all.' She glanced down her body, the length of her legs, to feet still quite delicious, and flexed her toes. Her eyes took on a preoccupied glaze.

The noise smashed back then. Catharsis. That was it. Catharsis.

I didn't mention, did I, that it was a largely young party – business trendies from Reeftown, a sprinkling of rent-a-car girls? Yet it wasn't a scramble or a plunge now into the baptismal properties of the pool, but rather an out-of-it sidle as people came dripping along the scootway feigning a need to dry out as they slid on a this or that; a yearning for liquor, as they fumbled towels or shirts over bare flesh, until in a short while most of the guests were at least half dressed and some were making time-to-be-going noises over which Bosie quacked with a kind of unhinged bounty.

Alone with her host on the raft, Mrs Waterman observed this, smiled gently then swam gracefully to the side where she dried herself lingeringly and thoroughly on a borrowed towel. Clothed once more, she turned elegantly to her hostess.

'Now,' she commanded firmly, 'I think I will have another gin.'

Has it happened?

Here we are and it's the same party and not the same party and only the dregs of us are left having a bash at the fish nibbles and the cheese. Brain heads off to the tape-deck and whacks in another cassette and swamped by sax we attempt normal things like riffling the polls prospects, swapping tax laments, until at twelve past one – I can swear to this precisely – I heard behind me the words, 'That Johnny Hodges sure is petals from blown roses on the grass.'

In the wide light of this statement I punctured my bubble of recluse snugness straight onto the mulch of cane-grass matting, leaning back as I was from the fag-snaffling ploys of some Pucci-clad rent-a-girl. ('I don't smoke,' I say, blowing smoke on her.) And I was straining to catch more of this unexpected rupture.

So I hear these words and I swing about and it's Brain all right, almost pulverised by grog, trying a few dance steps with Mrs Waterman. We're all pulverised except Mrs Waterman.

Brain staggers a little, his wife does keep plucking so, and scatters my whisky. 'Forgive,' he pleads drunkenly. 'Forgive for Johnny Hodges' sake. Listen! Oh, my God, will you listen a that!' Reeling with hand cocked to ear, catching the nightingale.

I've got a ton of absolution for this, too, and, granting the benedictus with an unsteady cross, I lug Miss Pucci from her chair and dump Brain into it. Mrs Waterman composes herself on a lilo by his side.

I must tell you about Brain. He is one of nature's dazzling failures, so injected with the fraudulent potency of his wild-cat schemes he is always on the verge of financial bliss or ruin. The only number he knows is 'millions'. He likes saying it. He has tried exporting goats to Arabia, pineapples to Hawaii, crayfish to Noumea. One project that worked was the buying up of railway tracks between two abandoned townships west of here. He carved the rails into telegraph pole lengths and sold them to a council with a big white-ant problem. Fired by his non-organic success, he developed a process for spraying the contents of waterless dunny pans with a plastic hardener that set like cement. 'A clear protective film,' he described it, 'that keeps down the flies.' Since the deposits also set like concrete in aspic, the problem was to find people prepared to dig them out.

After this failure he had a rage to die.

For two dreadful years he kept trying to kill himself. The first time he'd lain across the tracks of the Sunlander due to leave in five minutes. But there was a lightning strike he didn't know about and after three hours of waiting he was driven home by mosquitoes. The next time he tried it he slipped briskly over the side of his hired out-board at a nasty spot past the bay entrance and was picked up almost immediately by a prawn trawler coming unexpectedly from the north. 'God damn you to hell!' he was reported to have snarled as he dripped despairingly onto their decks. You see, his trouble was he wanted to go out with a roar of machismo. Not for him the pill bottle, the gas oven. 'Women's stuff!' he snapped. 'Bloody women's stuff!' He drove at trees. Only the car was wrecked. He jumped from buildings. There was none high enough in Reeftown. He tried throwing himself beneath the hooves of Queensland mounted police. The horses shied. Then two aunts he'd forgotten about died and

left him a small legacy. He snapped out of his death-wish in a
flash and here we are meeting while he's still on his high.

'Alfred,' he says, 'the Mouth, Tennyson.' He toasts
something and tries out some others. 'Cootie Tennyson.
Hey! How d'you like it? Cootie! Hotlips! Sweets!' He leans
heavily across Mrs Waterman. 'Hotlips Tennyson. I like that.
Jesus, I like it. Do you like it?'

'Very much.'

'And I like you very much. I like you for liking it.' He
begins a boozy conducting to the tape-deck. 'I like ole
Hotlips Tennyson and I like Alfred Fatha Hodges even
more.'

'I like Alfred Fatha Hodges too,' I say. 'Be-bop that
gentlier on the spirit lies.'

'Listen,' he says. 'Listen. I'm really onto something this
time, pal.' He has an arm round Mrs Waterman but is
holding me with his mariner's eye. Bosie is sitting on the lap
of one of the gate-crashers from the lugger who won't go
home. 'I've got this committee going, see? Top brass, mate.
Politicos. Academics. But the tops! It's a wonderful, it's a
huge concept.' He nods it into shape.

'For what?'

'Oh, my God! For what? he asks. For what! To stop the
brain-drain, that's for what. Keep the old genius located right
here in the sunburnt country. Let it drop the old fruit here,
see, not some ruddy foreign country that is for ever England.'

'You put that rather prettily,' says Mrs Waterman.

'I do put it prettily, don't I?' He gave her a spacious hug,
pushed out his juicy lower lip. Suddenly he thumped me on
the good leg. 'Keithy, baby, this is an enormous concept.
You gotta bloody believe me. I tell you, mate, I've been in
touch with the lot and confidentially' – he went confidential
– 'confidentially, the government has come to the party. Yes.

They've come to the party all right. They've promised me
half a million. Imagine that. Half a bloody million!'

'Brain!' Bosie cries petulantly. 'Brain, *please!*'

He didn't even hear and I could sense the dream-power
taking over. Johnny Hodges and his sax have soared right
out of space.

'It's rather difficult getting money from the government,
isn't it?' Mrs Waterman has brought the gin bottle over to the
table and is serving herself generously. She is monstrously
sober.

'Listen, sweetie,' Brain says, 'I have the Ministry of Science
interested, the leader of the Country Party, the vice-
chancellors of three universities' – he is up and away –,
'several judges. Oh God, yes! *They* see, I mean they really see
the magnitude of the thing. It's going to save the country
millions. Millions.' He wets his lip on the word. 'Could you,
my dear, hotlips, spare me one of those fags? Thank you.
This, pals, is going to be a tremendous, an absolutely bloody
tremendous undertaking.'

Mrs Waterman blows a perfect smoke circle that fits one of
her host's eyes like a monocle.

'A little vague, isn't it?'

His head wags sadly. He's hurt. He tells us again that he's
formed this committee and maybe he's right after all: we're a
great country for the maunderings of indirect action. His eyes
see chains of committees and sub-formations of the sub-
committees stretching into the wide brown distances and his
voice, enriched with the vibrations of delusion, comes across
the cultural void along with his salesman hand that smacks
mine enthusiastically and then flees to Mrs Waterman's
thigh.

'That Johnny Hodges!' he sighs, groping for her fingers
and then his glass.

Look at him! Can you see those doggy eyes, deeply, romantically brown? The tousled boy hair (he's only thirty-five give or take those suicides)? The glossy failure of him? It's all fantasy, this heroic taradiddle that gushes out, and I catch Mrs Waterman's eye and know she has discovered this as well. He's one huge monument of failure sustained by phoney dreams and it's sad, sad as his enthusiastic mug.

But he's bombing us with earlier ventures, and his figures sport dangling necklaces of zeros. 'Now that's doing well. Bloody well.' There's the word 'millions' again, the naughts drifting about us with the nebulous quality of snow, gathering, flake upon flake, about the committee and throwing darkness over the countries of his mind.

For a while I stop listening and think of another like him, a job changer of distinction, who's moved from computers to audits to insurance to pineapples and has buggered three crops. He tries again. His avocados get worm. He tries again, conventionally, and pushes pen for a tobacco company. He hates it. He tries again and is one of the middle-aged flower-people throwing pots on a home-made wheel. He makes one basic pot but in six sizes. He has one glaze. 'There is only one potter in this country,' he assures me with his soft nervous uh-uh that is meant to describe a circle of charming diffidence about a core of Jahveh-like ego. He means himself, of course, and this too is very sad, hearing his voice fade in inverse ratio to the crescendo of his fantasy. I bend to absorb each lie. 'Uh-uh they're ringing me from down south now for orders uh-uh – Perth even uh-uh.'

(My subject is self-delusion and the pity of self-delusion. Sorry, Wilf!)

I keep gazing into my glass, finding its concentricity both simple and delusory, the bubble-slice of something so fragile its moment keeps glancing off from me, out of reach, out of hearing. The other guests who have been swimming steadily downwards through transparent waves of claret are now seen through this circular translucence to fluctuate, shrinking and expanding like underwater creatures whose gesturings become the fin movement of infinite sluggishness, whose yowls scream silently through wall upon wall of glass. Miss Rent-a-girl has ousted Bosie from one luggerman's lap and is making sorties on the other, while Bosie, drunkenly disconsolate, wavers towards us.

'Brain,' she is pleading, 'Brain. Sing us something.'

This is a new Brain all right. I hadn't heard about this.

'You sing, do you?' Mrs Waterman asks.

'Me? Not really. Not for years.'

'Oh, but he does!' Bosie says. 'Ever so nicely. He was in opera once, you know.'

'Chorus,' says Brain. 'One season.'

'The naughty thing wouldn't practise, would you, Brain?'

'Jesus!' says Brain.

'Really?' Mrs Waterman asks, perking up. 'Really?'

'Back row of *Boris Godounov*.'

'Oh, do sing for us. Do.'

The luggermen start in then. 'C'mon, mate! Give us a tune. C'mon, feller!'

Roars. The limp smacking of hands. Brain staggers to his feet and begins divesting again. He tosses his shirt to his wife and does elbow circlings, mockingly, and takes in funny-man deep breaths. The tanned and hairy chest expands like a cartoon strong man's, while above him the patio fans describe slow fixed circles, centring our shambles.

Someone starts a slow thumping and the urging breaks out again; so reluctantly, grinning at Mrs Waterman, Brain stops his fooling, reaches over and takes her hand, raising it in a stage-pro gesture as he half-profiles to the noise and the yap.

'"Lindy,"' he begins softly, '"did yo hear dat mockin' bird sing las' night?"'

He increases the volume and bends the full force of his stupid failed eyes on Mrs Waterman. '"Lordy, it was singin' so sweet in de pale moonlight!"'

His voice is so rich, so naturally beautiful, the yappers are stilled. But Brain isn't aware of its beauty, I know it, for once again he's grinning like a goat, sending himself up as he does mammy gestures. '"Roun' dat ole magnolia tree,"' he sings, '"sang so sweet to you an' me. . . ."' On he sings. On. On. He misses a phrase now and then. We prompt the words. Once he almost loses the tune. But the voice! The depth! The resonance! Here it is – the one thing he can do and never talks about. He just doesn't know.

Petals from blown roses all over the drunken pool-way and the fans stir them; they settle, and I look across to Mrs Waterman who is kneeling, I swear, at his feet and bending, yes bending, in the simple curve of devotion.

6

Ladies Need Only Apply

6

I hear about Leo, Leo who worked for me once at the
motel: body-built, sang vilely, and vanished without trace.
   Tripp drops by with a coral trout he has hooked
somewhere up the coast and shoves its heroic bulk generously
into my deep-freeze, artistically withholding his predicate
until I produce the whisky. He's a great noser-out and
trundles his made-over jeep into all parts of the country,
stacking his boot with stories.
   'Gone to earth.' He's picking over a crab claw with the
scientific lust he brings to eating. 'I stumbled on him quite by
accident holed up about fifty miles from here. A very odd
set-up. Very. You ought to drop by.'
   Tripp understands my disenchantment, but he wants me
to accept it, all cheer and giggles. 'You'll never see the whole
of it,' he warns. 'Never. The versions are infinite.'
   Well, I'll accept that as I accept my little handicap, but as
the evening thins and the whisky level drops I persuade him
all the same to draw me a little map.
   I'll draw it for you.

'It's both too long and too short,' he uttered sententiously.
   'What is?'
   'Life.'

Inwardly she yawned, flapping an I've-heard-it-all-before hand over her mouth. Any minute now he'd trot out that old cliché about Tahiti: how did it go? A week is too long and a year isn't long enough. But he was threatening her with a fugue – *that* fugue – his only one, she estimated sourly, and she rose abruptly and, turning her back on him, padded out to the veranda. In his day he would have got more emotional mileage out of the Appassionata (played badly) than any man living and (by fifty-six, was it? -seven?) had declined the verb to lie in every mood and every tense of those moods, had slipped into an adroitness of supines and gerundives: in order to love, to be about to be loved, requiring to be loved.

He showered a few opening bars on her but she refused to succumb, sucking noisily at the last seeds in the passion-fruit, making kid noises, denying his nicely organised nostalgia at the teeth of his tinny grand. But there were the two of them, no denying it, hanging perilously together on an escarpment in the range in his dinge of a shack whose walls he had pansied with arrogant arrangements of dried fan-palm frond. '*Trachycarpus fortunei*,' he had said to her, botanically whimsical. 'Nature is the true artist.' And she had snorted inwardly again, 'Ah, crap!' But then they had been together only two hours and already, she assessed, drawing on her serial of calamities, she could calculate him to infinity.

Leaning her insolence back on the railing, she surveyed the inside of the room, repressing her list to interest, her eyes scuttling like sand-crabs over the adze-hewn benches, the dried grasses in bottles, his few books and a pile of music manuscript the hue of disappointment. And him. His looming bulk, his hairiness, the sweet-and-sour line of his mouth and a certain twitchiness (the nerves are where the heart is!), seemed themselves to reject the meditative calm jargon he had been peddling like some yoga rep. who hit the roads with his sample bag crammed to the brim with transcendental hogwash.

This is Thursday, she reminded herself. And that was when? Last Thursday? And now here? The hows of it were remarkable even for her, for whom time had done nothing but reposition the factors of error. Take the aimlessness of leave (too much of it) and middle-age (too much of that) and multiply. The product is bravado loneliness in a postcard tropadise (the greens are too green! the blues too blue!), another snappy set of casual wear expensively commenting on the thickening body beneath, and an eye, increasingly less casual, flicking, mock-flicking over the personal columns.

At first she kept telling herself she was only pretending, a joky research; but at the back of it all operated that mumbo-jumbo nerve that made her devour her stars for the morrow, pass over her tea-slops in cafés, hold out her palm, wear lucky dangles, drop coins in wishing-wells. Although she discounted the sexual adventure promised in trendier magazine columns ('I am not into leather and bondage!' she would assure her women pals with a giggle), she still ran her tired but hopeful eye down the more homespun cries in parish-pump journals where, she imagined, a more genuine anguish might be at work. There's nothing quite like recognising buddies in misfortune. My God, were some of them for laughs!

One particular notice should have halted her laughter.

Did, in fact, for a little, so that she re-read. And again. 'Companion housekeeper required for macrobiotic musician. Keep plus some wage. Interest in an alternative life-style, willingness to share musical and gardening interests essential. Genuine ladies need only apply.'

Rolling back on her beach towel, she had trilled with delight. Was she a genuine lady? Or genuine and a lady? The essential abstract? she wondered, viewing her carefully enamelled nails, the over-plump lurch of thigh. The misplaced adverb coupled with the pretentiousness of the demand pleased her enormously. 'Boy, could I handle him! I have only – no, merely – to apply!' she kept amusedly telling herself. 'And I get it. We get it. There'll be dozens and dozens of us.' And even as she rolled over again and nuzzled her face into her arm in a self-mocking attempt to stifle her mirth, she knew she would write.

The sun shouted at the sea and the sea kept repeating its answer, insidiously gentle, on the long beach north of town where, for a pointless month already, she had baited herself and lain unhooked beside a motel pool stuffed with ockers from the south. In a bleached way she had thought occasionally of the classrooms as a nightmare sequence on whose blackboard episodes she had stabbed sticks of chalk to death. The din of playground traffic rolled over the sand and the trimmed tourist grass with its heavy luncheon breath, and a word formed and kept re-forming in her mind against the sunny blood of her eyelids: no. No to that. Most definitely no.

And perhaps yes, microscopic but possible yes to this.

How estimate the stunning propositions of that advertisement's despair?

There were palms behind her and behind those palms there were over-ripe bracts of bougainvillea and behind that again the thundery blues of the tableland. Cracks between palm-frond were awash with sky so lucid, so resistless in its emptily spaced intentions, she knew she didn't have a hope.

She wrote. 'I must be,' she said to herself as she scrabbled for suitable words, 'crazy.' 'I must be,' she said to herself as she gummed down the envelope, 'out of my mind.' She licked the stamp. 'Mad,' she said to herself. And her mind stopped to catch its breath.

Stock-taking wasn't too good in the motel evenings, alone with the cold cream and the re-plays on telly. She felt, at times, despairingly, that she was one of those desperate women who infest reef waters from March to October. 'The stingers move out,' the locals used to say, 'and the birds move in. You get bitten either way.'

She wasn't conservative. She wasn't really dull. She was simply – well, let's put it this way – forty-two. And too often lately her nights had been a chop ('Got to keep that strength up!' – but for what?) or two poached eggs, or a concert series ticket when she cut a safe dash in something long and shapeless and her ear-lobes killed her with unaccustomed trinkets. Once, midway, she had been married, but only for half an hour as it were. At the end of a year he had gone with such flatness of purpose she had barely noticed. One night he had said, 'Darling, I'm just going to put the garbage out', and had never come back.

For a week after she had written and was finally beginning to forget she had, she lay by the pool revving up her tan or wandered disconsolate along the sand front where sometimes she stopped for a bit and built rather lop-sided little sand-castles. When she dug doors in them, the sand wept briefly and collapsed. Everything was like that for her. Some humble erection. The totter. The rupture. The flattened surface.

That she received a reply to her monstrously coy note surprised her. She read it trying not to feel eager, and the old pulse, the old excitation, began its idiot pounding. She let the letter dangle from her fingers and waved it delicately against the fact of five months more of leave. The perimeters of that time became space and the edges of space melted and broke, desert-fashion. 'Naughty!' she chipped herself. 'You are a naughty, foolish thing.'

Nevertheless she thrust back her self-queryings and dressed

with extra care for the meeting. Ah! all those other meetings, dressing, extra care. The dabs of something not quite innocuous at vital spots, the straining muscle torture for the rear and profile glimpse which mirrored nothing of the inner suspense yet caught her in a dangerous hall of mirrors with herself still straining, turning, dabbing in an unending colonnade of doppel-gangers.

He was much older than she had expected.

So was she.

He sported a bushwacker beard of streaked white and his bald skull had a leathery and repulsive tan to it. She gave him an extra point for height but subtracted two for a something in the eyes she could not read. There had been a shouting silence while her fingers dabbled about in her curls. Then he waded in.

'Miss Klein?'

'Mr Stringer?'

It was a relief to shake hands, establish formality while ferociously her mind tossed around negations: I've never . . . you mustn't think . . . don't imagine . . . this is not really like. . . . She said none of those things and he watched her saying none of it. He appeared, in fact, indifferent to the situation and asked carelessly would she like to sit in the restaurant attached to the motel. Would he care for tea? she asked. He didn't drink it. Coffee perhaps? Never. Well, something a little – she hesitated.

'I eat natural foods only,' he said. 'Actually I just thought you might like to have a bit of a talk first.'

She was about to agree when he went on, 'But if you prefer we'll take the run straight back and have a look at the place.'

'Whatever you –' She became firm. 'I think I will have tea.'

So they sat and inspected each other and he sipped water while she messed around with her tea and he repeated his remark, 'I eat natural foods only', tempering it with a smile this time. She responded understandingly. Natural foods need only apply. 'Nuts. Fruit. Never meat, you understand. Lots of vegetables, raw. And I rarely cook. Cooking destroys essentials.' His hands emptied out something useless and she wondered if that last dab of blusher had destroyed her own. Hating herself, – and she didn't know this was to be a pattern – she found she was clucking phrases like 'You're right, of course', 'There's a lot to be said for it.'

'There is everything to be said for it.' There was only the merest adumbration of menace. 'Everything.'

His blatant belief in his rightness was affecting her like sunstroke. She knew, oh she knew already, she had made a mistake. It all seemed like a bad joke, one gone wrong, whose only redemption would be the later jocular recounting, the wacky thrill of the send-up; but then the very thought of later was a stopper in itself, so it was inevitable when once more he suggested they drive up the plateau that she should groggily accept.

The floor of the panel-van was scattered with empty grain sacks. She wedged her smashing new sandals between two drums of honey and cranked down the window clumsily. My God! she thought. Madness!

He had watched her expressionlessly for a moment and then gave a smile of such warmth she was charmed.

'Easy. Easy does it.' He leant across her and finished the winding.

This was the point, she decided, for a loud and firm announcement that never, not ever, had she resorted to the dubiousness of advertised friendship, and she half-opened her mouth for confession when he anticipated her.

'I get the feeling you're a bit of a newcomer to this.'

'This what?'

'Well, this sort of thing. Ring up a pal.' He switched on the ignition.

'You're an old hand?'

'I didn't say that.'

They drove steadily north in silence, reef waters to the right and hills pressing hard on the left.

'Mr Stringer –'

'The name is Leo.'

'Leo, then. Tell me –'

'And yours is Sadie, isn't it? I think we might as well skip the formal bits.'

This was the point where she always played it wrong. She decided on smiling silence.

'Is Klein your married name?'

That jolted her. 'I don't recall saying I was.'

'But you were.' His emphasis hardly needed an answer and anyway he was smiling again, tricking curves on the road as well.

'Well, yes. For a while.'

'What was it?'

'What was what?'

'Your married name.'

'I don't remember,' she replied. 'Were you? Married I mean?'

'Now and then,' he said and roared with laughter.

She was unable to inspect the random creases of his amusement but recalled the rinsed quality of his eyes and her bleakness returned. On the steering-wheel his hands observed a blunt competence and, watching the careless strength of them, her folly appalled her, erupted into misgiving made positive by the loneliness of the coast road where, by now, they had lost sight of the sea. That movement of water-light had bolstered her but the taciturn quality of the hill scrub into which the car had turned made her belly twitch.

It remained taciturn for miles. Occasionally the man beside her put a question, made a comment, but each question or statement was strangely tangential. There she was, a woman of non-radiant years bashing away into distance now mid-field with a stranger in a game whose rules, this time, she didn't know.

Even the soft-edge warnings were gone.

They'd left the bitumen and some of the heat as well as the road lumbered up into the hills between rain-forest so chancelled with trees that the mid-morning took on the dreamy airless implications of late afternoon. There was only the car's panting.

'You must be pretty isolated,' she suggested, partly to challenge the thwack in the blood.

He glanced at her and knew she was regretting her stupidity.

'Pretty much. It's the way I like it. Cities are filth.'

Funnily enough the violence of his last emphasis reassured her, was a pattern-part of what his appearance seemed to claim. The stickiness under her fingers dried on the dilly-bag straps she had been clutching like a life-belt.

A down-slope now. After the climb west from the coast the van took a set of ruts along an old snigging trail heading east again and there came a sense of half-tone as the trees panned out, demobilised finally by a broad clearing on the remote side of which, through groined intervals in the plateau scrub, the sea cried its permanent name.

It was a blueprint for a slovenly Eden.

An intransigent fecundity dominated two shacks which were cringing beneath banana clumps, passion-vines, grana-dillas. One was a patchy timber affair of cedar planking, and across from it, connected by a log bridge that spanned a steeply banked creek, was a smaller building plastered with mud and pebbles. And everywhere flowers and leaves exploded with tropic swagger.

She tried to repress her gasp, but it was too much for her and she said so.

'Is it?' He seemed amused and then he was out of the car, slamming the door behind him and leaving her to fight the stiff handle on her own side. He watched her till she made it and for a moment she hated him, blindingly, as she cracked her knuckles and felt the pain shiver right up her arm. 'Christ!' she said under her breath, and then the door gave, almost flinging her out, and she had to chew up the yelp she wanted to give and offer instead a smile, bluffing but askew.

It was wasted. He'd turned already and she could only follow his indifferent back as he stepped high and light down the track between the papaw-trees to the front of the bigger shack where he stood waiting ('Tapping his bloody foot!' she would tell them later), a meaty bulk of a man, cross-hatched by stratagems of light and shadow that made the him of the fellow even more elusive. But pain had damped down her fright.

The house was instantly knowable. There were only three walls, the front merely a veranda'd extension of the inner room, unenclosed but so massed with plants and streamers of vine it seemed stubbornly to be the bush itself.

She'd hardly begun to say 'Why?' when he thumped in an explanation.

'The heat. We do it this way for the heat. If you position it right it doesn't catch the weather. Not much, that is. And it's a hell of a lot cooler.'

She nodded, still rubbing her knuckles. 'Yes. Yes, of course. But your things? How do you lock up?'

'You must be from town, Miss Klein!' he said, mocking. 'I

don't have many – what you call *things*. Anyone after my few
scraps'd have to come a damn long way. They'd have to be
really looking, wouldn't they?'

The more he out-manoeuvred her, the more the dislike
settled in, became familiar. Why, we could almost be friends,
she thought angrily, regaining her irony. Her hand throbbed
but reassured her like a known part of her track work-out.
'Oh, God!' she thought bitterly and said, 'It's enchanting.'

It was true that in her sense he hadn't many things. The
shack was one yawning room about twenty feet square,
bullied by a very large piano set well back but still
dominating a bed, a couple of cane chairs and some kitchen
still-life. The walls bristled with fan-palm and on a table near
the piano were some lumpish carvings, animal-human
hybrids of lustreless black. Her eyes were drawn to their
unpleasantness first.

'Genuine,' he offered almost contemptuously. 'None of
your tourist gallery trash.'

She could sense him wanting her to bleat phrases of
adulatory rubbish and when she did, inspired by her dislike,
she achieved an unwanted victory, for suddenly he became
more talkative. He picked up one carving after another,
perhaps trying to throw her with their sexual hyperbole, but
by now she felt in control and only half-listened as he told her
where he'd got it, what it meant. But she fractured the mood
by wandering away from him to the piano, and he offered
her a drink.

'Only herbal, I'm afraid.' He challenged her with a shine of
teeth through beard. 'No concessions, not even for visitors.'

She struck a note. The sound was plangent, distorted by
age and years of damp, and the pretentiousness of the piano's
bulk alongside its quality again pleased her sense of irony.
Why, swinging round to observe his idiot seriousness

watching her, she felt better already. Better better better. 'Please,' she said. 'Straight.'

As she sat sipping at the cloudy, faintly acrid mixture he'd poured her, he began looking her over more closely, charting her quality. She was big-boned and probably strong and, despite the enamelled properties of her, he was thinking, not the fool he might have wanted or the incompetent he would reject. He'd learnt during a lifetime spent poking around in odd corners to assess malleability to the last submissive quiver. The volatility of her nature and a certain melting flesh he observed within the opening of her shirt challenged his creativity. He began to talk about himself, opening with king's pawn, about his private theories, his dogmatisms, unapologetic and absorbed.

Miss Klein, playing along, tried to throw herself into the spirit of it, looking for amusement; but there was too much of it. In for a brisk plunge, and there you were dog-paddling desperately through glue. When at last he had gone to the pensioner piano, trying another gambit, she'd headed for the veranda and tried listening to the view; but he was beside her within minutes and to her shock she found that without turning she was conscious of his body.

'Well, now,' he asked, looking hard at her above his glass rim, above the herbal trickle that ran yellow into his beard, 'what do you think of the place?'

Her hesitation amplified and echoed in the big dim barn. It was almost scrupulously clean, she had noticed, and in its exotic way disturbingly neat. That note she had struck – had it pulled apart regiments of permitted sound? For its aftermath still seemed to rock the air despite the fugue. She regretted that note.

She looked back inside. Sun was clouting the room with light through a western window. There was a smell of soap and leaves.

Gush seemed to have seeped away with her newly found indifference.

'It's very different.'

'Compared with what?' He didn't want her to reply but drummed out a few bars with his fingers on the rail beside her. 'You're wondering,' he went on, not looking at her but at his practising fingers, 'just why I advertised. Aren't you?'

'You could ask me the same.'

'I know why *you* did.' He paused to let it reach home. Check. Rightly, he estimated, she would understand all the elements of affront. 'I've tried to explain to you why I'm here. I've some income, not much, but some. I don't need the cities any more. I haven't needed them for a long time. I need a hand, not just for town trips – I do hate the bloody place – to pick up essentials but with the garden. You won't believe it, but I can't keep up to the watering in summer. It takes a good two or three hours every day. And there are other things.' He raised his eyebrows comically and won her for a moment. 'I need someone to moan to. I wanted,' he said practising a diminuendo, 'to have someone to share it with.'

'You mean you get lonely?'

'Sometimes.' She couldn't believe it.

'Why a woman?' she asked with the faintest touch of tartness.

'Why not? They can be – or so I've found – less difficult.'

And before she could negotiate that he'd steered her back into the room again to have another go at the herbal stuff and a dish of cheese and fruit he'd put on the table. Harmonics still hung in the air.

The hows of it. And now there were the two of them dangling perilously together and heat-impressed like flowers in some book to wilt in each other's pages.

'There's another thing,' he said.

'What?'

He regarded her hands with the too-long nails on the too-plump fingers. Something checked him.

'I'll let you know as we go. If we go.'

'I hate mysteries,' she said. 'What should I say?'

'You don't say anything.' Her antagonism became an instant goad. 'Not yet, eh? Would you like to see the rest of the place? Your part of it. If you're interested.'

It was much like his, only smaller, barer; but at the rear and awash with papaw light there was a tiny shower-room under the water-tank.

'It's spartan,' she commented.

'You did say,' he challenged her, 'you were after something different.'

They paused on the centre of the bridge and she mopped at some of the afternoon which was running down her face.

'I did, didn't I?'

Her irony showed and he felt she was slipping away from him. He gave her a marvellous smile. 'You could give it a try, you know. Both of us. Testing. It will be a help, especially now I have pupils.'

'Pupils?' The merest pucker on her face, but he caught it.

'Only a couple. I'm really too far out. And then I'm not interested in numbers, you understand. Only quality.'

He managed to make the prerequisite sound like a compliment to her.

She looked back at the shacks. She looked down at the garden and the barbaric leaf shape and sheen with its succulent pulpy cannibal gobbling of heat and moisture. Impossible. She looked back at him and he loomed across a landscape of crowded playgrounds and empty rooms and the brutality of the sameness that had leached her out. It was still impossible.

Overhead, a small Beechcraft droned in from the north,

swinging in closer, low, too close, dipped one saluting wing
and swung away again down the coast.

Mr Stringer was waving a casual arm. The gesture was
attractively *dégagé* as if some divine prompter was hooting at
her from the wings.

The first of it for her was both easy and hard.

A week softened their wariness and when he found her to
be more competent than he had hoped he would surprise
himself pausing to observe her slogging away in some corner
of the garden. The utter difference in life-style gave her much
inward amusement and she hummed 'If my friends could see
me now', dragging hoses round the lower acre. Stripped to
shirt and shorts, the muck off her face, she revealed a sturdy
handsomeness that interested the watching man, who
conceded a blooming he might some time desire to control.

The days for her stretched into an endurance of muscle and
became one enlarged aching scar on an endless calendar of
surprising dawns and exhausted evenings. The tropic blaze,
of course, did not diminish, and the week or so of trial she had
secretly allowed herself for laughs extended as she discovered
he was tolerable simply as a present chunk of male whose
remoter coastline she found herself wanting to chart.
Although he knew she had taught, she refrained from telling
him she was on leave and allowed him to believe her retired
and independent. As well, she refused wages, and kept one
economic jump ahead.

The second mandate came within a week.

He was a singer, an achromatic baritone, despite the thick-
set chest, and had once grubbed out an undignified living for
a short time singing ballad spots round clubs in the south. He
had little talent, even Miss Klein could see; but like most

singers remained unaware. As she spaded and mulched and watered, unending skeins of arpeggios and scales, ravelled phrases and dangerously sustained top notes, blew through the garden clearing and out to sea. When he learnt she played a little, he set her to work with him, rostering practice hours for her to work on song accompaniments while he was out of the shack and doing the heavier work on a section he was clearing. His voice, she thought amusedly, and the piano were a perfect match. Sometimes she had a vision of herself in this improbable situation, and the folly of it set her teeth on edge until she reminded herself it was only for giggles, my God, it was – and in any case, in *any* case, she was waiting for something. What that something was she refused to examine.

Sometimes, bluffed by the distances he set between them, she found herself deliberately seeking his approval, and felt he was turning her into one of her own pupils, eager to be noticed.

Lately, on her way back from the lower clearing where she had been deep-watering the younger trees, she came upon him stripped and showering lustily beneath the tank-stand. Anyone could see he was in splendid shape. If this were the awaited moment it confused her, and during her hesitation he swung round to face her and slowly, deliberately, not taking his eyes off her, raised one arm and began lathering an armpit. Awkwardly she jerked away.

The second time it happened he simply stood still; and there were the two of them staring at each other until he gave her a scant smile that lost itself in hair.

Now and again a visitor (pupils, he said) shoved a battered Kombi down the by-road, and as she wilted in the afternoon siesta she would hear from the other shack across the creek talk and interrupted musical clauses that flowed as part of the heat: both stunned her. There was a singer (softly young and large-eyed with a voice like a flute) and a pianist who played with greater bombast than the master. Should Sadie surprise the singer's arrival when she was on one of her compost-lugging missions in the top section, she would be given a flitter smile (eyes shifting shyly from their own morsel of goodwill) and endure an odour of resentment like part of the weather.

The piano pupil didn't speak at all. His sombre, good-looking face inspected hers briefly, made some quick calculation, then turned away. He would drive up, park, play savagely for an hour as if he wanted to kill the piano, then leave.

Leo was vague about his students as he was about his own musical background. She felt, from the few facts he tossed her like placatory biscuits ('The boy? Galipo – some lawyer's kid. Bit of a smart-arse who needs sitting on hard') . . . that he'd always been one for the fantasy of living rather than the actuality. In her resenting moments (My God! Why do I stay?), she wanted to open up on him with acid truths.

'You can't sing,' she longed to say, 'and your playing isn't much better. You're a bag of wind.' But then he would charm her with a sudden warmth or enthusiasm, so that she was kept swinging in a maddening emotional suspension through which the vision of him beneath the shower ballooned and retreated.

After a month she noticed he was managing to manipulate her absence on student afternoons.

'Need a bit more kero,' he'd say. 'How about trotting down to town for it?' Or, 'We're running light on flour. And there's a couple of other things while you're about it. There's a part for the generator. I'll write it down.'

As she banged away sulkily over the dirt road she pondered on the girl, Flute, speculated irritably as to what they did when she was not there, how Flute comported herself in that Rousseau landscape, the tiger in the leaves. But it was Sadie who was tiger.

Reduced to mere clippings of dialogue over the evening chess-board. Lack of detail was beginning to make her prowl while frustration made her want to eat him whole.

In the fifth week, as they were sitting together after tea and just as she had decided once more that she must leave, he deposited on the back of her hand one of the rare pats that so whetted her. Mosquito-coils smoked all round them. The distant sea had become slate. Leo crushed a couple of March flies to death on his splendid mahogany thigh and looked at her speculatively.

'I think you're getting to like it here now.'

'Why, yes. I think I do. At least I'm getting used to it.'

'Are you getting used to me?'

She chewed her answer. Was this the point where grace ran out of the soul? There was menace in his jocular question, but the hand still lay like an oblation on her own.

'You're a man of many parts,' she said. 'They take some getting used to.'

He was pleased with that. He rose and stood above her with a curious inspecting gaze she resented, and she sullenly dropped her eyes to find them on a level with his thighs. She had never seen so much hair. She swerved, bending back in the cane lounger, to be assaulted again by weather-stained and bulging shorts, the shining breasts, and the stink of sweat that came with him: blocking out thought now till she found his face and saw nothing but the white of teeth behind beard. Suddenly she resented his smile, his continual unsmiling smile; and suspecting mockery she sat up and pettishly looked down at herself. He was nudging her bare ribs with his knee.

'You're fining down, Sadie. Looks a lot better. A very lot better.'

The knee stayed.

It was true. Six weeks had removed the blubber. There was a deal of tan. The lumpish excitement that grabbed her took her fingers to her face and she tracked its planes vaguely, dragged at her unbarbered hair that hung freer, oilier, in sweaty elf-locks about her shoulders.

'You think?'

He watched closely as her hands moving humbly down her hips recognised this and stirred by her diffidence, for it was diffidence he wanted, he bent over and seized her. His mouth seemed to be biting into her neck, but she could hear words being mumbled and she dragged herself back from him to hear him say, 'You've lost the patent-leather look, Sadie. You look like a woman.' His eyes were insolent and then his mouth was back again, biting that smile into her throat.

Her vanity revolted. She tensed and shoved at him.

'You mean I wasn't before?'

'Not much.'

Her fury wrestled and his arms seemed to be everywhere hands, mouth: the settee overturned into a silent and massive struggle that writhed across the floor of the shack until she bit him savagely and he let her go with a cry.

'That wasn't in the agreement,' she gasped.

He glared at her, panting. 'Maybe not. Sorry.'

The ripe stink of them yowled; but he was shrivelled and furiously bounced up to take his rage down the steps into the dark garden.

Of course he punished her after that in a variety of ways, but he didn't suggest she leave and, contrarily, she didn't offer. There were earlier and earlier risings, brutally hearty and notched out on the pearl of the mornings with walloping wakey cries: 'Upski, Sadie! Outski! Water gir-hir-hirl! [sung badly] Where are you hi-yi-ding?' Caught in mid-note by her while his eyes stayed hard.

As well, he stopped sending her on fake errands when Flute came sauntering into the jungle.

'Hullo, Sadie!' Flute would trill these days, dawdling deliberately as Sadie savaged pest on the soursops. The girl would twist long strands of hair round a thoughtful finger then give her neat peasant-wrapped bottom a little shake before turning to Leo who always stood waiting for her on the veranda, stripped to the waist, smiling as he watched the two of them.

He was making Miss Klein (and lately, now, he called her that) aware that it was not only voice he moulded.

For he had, not long after their angry struggle, stationed her (with geographic cunning) to set out some silver-beet in a patch he had dug just below the window of the bigger shack. She was half-way through her task when she became aware that the singing had stopped and they could now be heard working at pleasure of another kind. Their penultimate groans slammed her hand-fork into the damp soil and propelled her nauseated lust into a run – tripping, stumbling, over the foot-bridge to her room where perplexity and desire spreadeagled her across the seething quilt.

It was still close enough to hear Flute's final gasp. 'Sod you!' Sadie whispered into the quilt. Over and over: 'Oh, sod you, sod you, sod you.'

I would go, she kept telling herself now, if I had any pride. But had she ever gone, ever dodged the ignominy of dismissal? Genuine and luscious tears of indulgence washed twenty years of dismissal down her streaked cheeks. It was as if she were frozen into patterns of martyrdom that insisted she had no pride at all as her last Max-Factored-skin was peeled away. There was only Sadie Klein of riper – let's still not quibble about numbers – years pared down to the sore parts and lugging a need that was always charged over-weight.

Tea was silent that night as she sulked to his triumphant crunching, crumbs stuck arrogantly all through his beard.

He was paddling about in his soup.

'Could have been colder!' he criticised, chucking a gob of cream into the bowl and stirring. Cheap beatitudes sang through his body as he squatted half naked in the heavy vine-dark of the veranda eating noisily and smacking the moths that kept rushing to die in lamp-light. The night outside was bulky with unbroken rains and noisy with tree and creek.

'It's you,' she said bitterly. 'You'd warm anything.' And she snatched her plate up and went back to her shack and finished eating alone. But he still intruded, for after she'd gone he started singing as he clashed plates together in the sink and his voice seemed to bore right into the marrow of her solitariness.

These days as he worked he sang a great deal with a challenging insolence that appeared in his swinging walk. His voice seemed to be thickening as phlegmily as the cloud-piles massing up and moving over before the wet. Dragging hoses down the far end of the clearing she would hear and wonder why it ate at the pith of her, and she checked off again the days left – but for what? Perhaps she dreaded an end to hatred. Yet it all seemed an exercise in paradox. Now it was she who, filled with eager dislike, put the chess-board away after tea and suggested a song or two; who blundered into muddles of small-talk, abhorring the vacuum; who began once more, but delicately, to make up her mouth.

133

He listened to this and he looked at this. And he smiled.
He began digging easements for the wet and he went on
singing in his clogged voice.

One day, the day Flute was expected for her lesson, Sadie
set herself to work by the entrance gates where they were
trying to establish an arcade of sorts sculptured out of guinea
vine. Ripe for assault of a spiritual kind, she leant her lip-
sticked insolvency on an impudent spade and watched as the
van pulled in. She smiled. Learning, she smiled.

Flute came round the front of the van.

'Hullo,' she said, curious, hugging her tattered alibi of
sheet-music to a chest which, Sadie noticed with malice, was
less emphatic than her own.

Sadie didn't answer. Oh, the power of it! But she smiled.
She smiled and smiled and went on spading the dirt with an
abstracted unawareness. She smiled again when Flute went
past an hour later; but this time the girl kept her eyes down
and pretended not to see.

The defiance tasted of love as well.

When she went back to the shack to prepare the evening
meal, she was most aware of him in her eye's oblique and
sensitive corner that kept seeing him fifty yards off working
beneath the trees. His sun-blackened shoulders shone wet, his
body, she understood with corrupting pleasure, bent,
straightened, bent, straightened with the rhythm of verse.
Should she practise the indifference of the smile upon him?
Their problem was, of course, her refusal to be humbled.

That night, as he took his place at the table, her resolution
failed. She could not offer the smile. She was too consumed
and, instead, her hand, impelled by sexual gloom, hovered
then rested on his. He watched it with some amusement, then
pushed it delicately aside.

'That isn't quite enough,' he said.

'What do you mean?'

'Oh, not the what of it,' he replied, reaching over for the bread. 'The how. The how.'

'I don't understand.' She was dying inwardly again.

'Oh, you will. You most certainly will.'

Back in her own shack, she examined and re-examined the remark, her mind refusing whole octaves of possibility as she heard him crack his way up a scale. She lay down, trying to munch away at a book; but it was hopeless, and as she slammed it down she heard his car roar away across its pages.

Still insomniac when he returned hours later, she saw the headlamps cutting slices into the dark of the unlined walls and it was only after she heard his feet creak lightly up the stairs and across his veranda that she let go the fear she had been hugging in the thick darkness of the rain-forest and fell asleep.

'Aren't you going to ask?' he nagged next morning.

She stared past him at the glutinous green.

'Ask what?'

'Where I went last night.'

Her confidence had returned. 'No. Did you go somewhere?'

'Oh, come on, Sadie. You're dying to.' He swallowed a raw egg oyster-fashion.

Her rage was so athletic with bile she swayed.

'All right,' she conceded, her eyes pasted on him. 'Where?'

'To get a bit of tail.' He shouted with laughter at the sight of her face.

She began, 'I think I must tell you –'

'What must you tell me, Sadie? What must you bloody tell me? What did you expect me to say? Look, I'll tell you something, you member of a virgin breed screwed up with your wants and your don't wants. Oh, yes, I know you're not a virgin in the literal sense. Don't wince. You don't like words like virgin, do you? Virgin virgin virgin virgin.' He sang it, scale-form. 'But in the real sense you are a puking bloody-minded product of every bloody-minded piece of published magazine garbage that ever was. Giant tips humming with green bottle flies. And the flies all have their big compound eyes beautifully made up. And while they lay their little corrupt eggs, that make-up mustn't be disturbed. My God, it mustn't.'

'Mustn't be disturbed!' he sang and cracked another egg into his hand and swallowed it.

'You sing flat,' she said.

He flinched as if she'd hit him. They stared at each other in a terrible silence and her words kept echoing round the room.

'I think I'd better leave.' She waited.

He seemed to recover his humour all of a sudden. 'Leave?' he said. 'Leave? Just because I've told you a few good-humoured home truths? We both have. Where's that logic of yours, eh? The very thing that attracted me about you. Where's that genuine search for another life-style? You didn't like the one you had, you've told me often enough. No, Sadie, my dear, you won't leave. Because I won't help you to and more fundamentally than that – you don't want to. And I like,' he added with cunning and wanting to gain the upper hand, 'to have you around.'

'Oh, my God!' she cried, flummoxed.

The day moved into its pattern.

In the new clearing by the creek where he had felled most of the big stuff, she attacked the landscape with anger, grubbing out the wait-a-while and bush-sword that was still guzzling round the stumps. Fifty yards off he worked with a hand axe. Clump clump, persistent, driving. The mail flight north went overhead and dipped its wing to his wave, and the small circle created by his circling arm widened, expanded, and flowed out to break on the mild timeless edges of the grove. She was slipping into infinity, she thought, unable to reason beyond this moment of the cracking back, the shoulder tug, the sweat drench between the breasts.

That afternoon she went down to the creek where it entered the forest, stripped, and floated in the water-hole. She wanted silence so she could think it out; but as she floated under the forest canopy she found there was nothing to think about or salvage in the coolness that reduplicated whatever it was he was playing up at the shack; so that the run of notes brothered the creek, moved into it, into the white blur she had become.

After, as she dried herself, there were leeches, blood, tears.

Humbled, she asked that night, 'What was it you were playing this afternoon?'

'You liked it, Sadie?'

She was afraid of tricks. After all, she was trying to atone.

'Yes. Yes, I did. Very much.'

'And what did you like about it?' His glinting eye challenged her. The tea-towel dangled from her hand, hopeless. There was a trick.

'I'm not sure,' she said. 'I just liked. Something. The creek in it.'

'The creek in it?' He made her sound foolish. Wait, she told herself. Wait for the smile.

'Yes.' It sounded stupid now, not beautiful as she had intended. And he was smiling again. 'I wouldn't mind hearing it once more.'

'Wouldn't you?' he said, enjoying her penance. 'To tell the truth, I don't feel much like playing this evening. It's been a heavy day. I think I'll turn in early. And you'd better catch up on some sleep, too.'

'Oh, my God!' she cried. 'We're getting nowhere at all, are we?' He was silent. 'Do you hear? It's simply getting nowhere. Nowhere. It's a waste of time. To tell the truth' – it was unconscious parody –, 'a total goddam waste of time and we both know it. Have known for weeks.'

'I thought you'd never notice,' he replied, not bothering with the whack her mouth showed but becoming, despite the lighted room, part of the dark outside it.

Even Sadie marvelled at her capacity for punishment as she shone her torch back across the foot-bridge. Even when spoken good-nights had failed her they still wanted to be uttered.

The papaw-trees clustered with fruit now smelled thickly in air still and loud with the held-back water of the wet. As again she lay sleepless on the tumbled bed, the night was so motionless she could hear the crackle of turned pages of the week-old paper he was reading. She became all ear in the weighty dark, a tightened membrane against which the stir of his hair, his lips, the unbent muscles of his fingers, lost their silence and made monstrous drumming.

Later that evening the clouds broke.

Into further days. Into further nights. They were all latticed with water.

There could be no question of her leaving now, for the next morning his crackling radio told them they were cut off at the bottom of the range road. In the short sun-dazzles that came between the striding rain, Leo would dig the easement run-offs deeper, splaying out the storm-water drains that ran from both shacks to the creek. Flute and the pianist stopped coming and there were the two of them still hanging perilously together on this escarpment in the range, forced to share the same bitter herbal quaffs and chess games she was no longer careful to lose. Monsoon clouds kept hauling their freight from the north as the sticky heat of the day glued the landscape into a ripening circle that sprouted more trees, more fruit. Pulp. Pulp and mould.

The heaviest rain seemed to come at night. Sadie would sprawl naked on her bed deafened by the crash of water on tin, watching the incessant silver of it in the lamp-glow, cut off, she knew now, from the world. The din of playground traffic no longer rolled across the clearing; the luncheon breath could not penetrate this grille, this mesh, so tough it became a caul. At times, in the heart of a downpour, the small sweating room was like an air-bubble trapped under-sea and to move into the outer world would be to drown.

Between one fall and the next, landscape was sponge, aching with wet.

On the fourth morning in, under the gust of it, she found that the creek was only a few inches below the strap-log of the bridge.

He was inclined to grunt when she first told him, but later commented almost genially as they had breakfast, 'Quite an adventure for you!' Full of nods and becks and bloody wreathed smiles, she thought sourly. 'Don't you like all this?' Gesturing at the weeping landscape. 'It makes me feel marvellous.'

She stared out at climate-shock. 'It's too much. Too hard. Too sudden.'

'But it's always like this. Every year. We're in for weeks of it now,' he said maliciously. 'Surely you're not frightened by the prospect! You're like all southerners, and when I say southerners I mean anyone below the tropic. They throw a mickey the first time they cop it. The Noah syndrome.'

'Did you say weeks?'

'Weeks. Ten. Twelve. Not much we can do about the garden for a bit, but that's the beauty of it. Enforced contemplation – for you, Sadie, anyway. It'll do you good. By God, it's doing me good.'

And it was. Each sodden dawn he did elaborately detailed flexing exercises until his body ran with the sweat the garden once gave him, displaying his body as he might one of his carvings. She watched until his fitness savaged her and she could watch no longer.

'Join in! You'll get 'the old flab back if you don't.'

'The mind's got it already,' she commented softly. Not aggressively. Just commented. But he didn't hear, was away on body presses which he performed with the dedication of a revivalist. Was he scourging the flesh, she wondered, or perfecting it?

During the second week of rain an electric storm clattered in from the sea and spent itself on the ridges. Lightning sabred the open side of her shack with primitive switches of high white dazzle that cut the dark wide open. She rigged up a blanket from a cross-beam as a sort of screen and lay sleepless before these summer movies and tried not to think about Leo. This can't keep up, she told herself. A couple of weeks and I'll be gone. She had a vision of the glade as some Druidic circle, herself spreadeagled in the centre of her humiliation, the permanent, the undying victim for whom the factors of error had now become the ever-raised, the never-falling knife. The sudden shock of the thought that perhaps this was her final destiny shot her upright, fully alert; and despite the rattle of water and the biblical thunder she caught the sound of tinny patches of music blowing across and through, contrapuntally, not in twin frenzy but in a kind of ironic – My God, could he really be playing Mozart at a time like this? – comment: the sort of opponent in debate who quibbles about your grammar or pronunciation.

'You bastard,' she breathed into her clammy hands. 'You arrogant bastard. I hate you.'

The foot-bridge was under by morning and the creek a thirty-foot spasm of sulky brown, biting at the roots of the first papaw planting up by the other shack. She called Leo's name once, twice; then she saw him come sauntering onto his veranda naked and polished once more with sweat as if he'd just finished a work-out. He waved a casual hand and shouted something.

Wind smothered his words.

'What?' She had to yell twice.

She could see him cup his hands about his mouth to call.

'I said you'll have to sit it out for a bit. Don't try to get across.' She could tell he was smiling. 'It'll probably go down in a few hours if the weather eases.' He appeared to be inspecting her reactions with interest. 'Got any tucker?'

'Not much. There's a bit of fruit here and I can make tea,' she called.

He yelled back, 'You do that.'

'What if it gets worse?' Her words blew out to sea. She called out again, but he only waved and went back inside.

The whole sky was rioting.

Throughout the day she glimpsed him throughout the blotching green of the shifting trees as he moved the chairs on his veranda back in from the galing wet. Every surface absorbed and sucked the sky down into it. She measured hours by pots of tea – that and the constant checking of the flood levels and trying to catch something on her battery radio. Its static exhausted her, and as the lead of the day-rain became the slippery black-silver of night she submitted, went out to the furthest edge of the veranda, and cried his name over and over against the hurlings of the wind.

Nothing. His name boomeranged back into her mouth, was tasted and flung out again. Still nothing.

The water was racing eagerly about the piles of the shack and she gave what seemed to be a scream for him; but although there was no answering shout it seemed for a moment that she glimpsed him, a flitter of shadow, across the path of his light.

Later she went to press down the switch of her own lamp but the room remained dark. Shaken, she flicked it again. Again. The power was gone; and as she recalled the rackety generator he housed behind the main shack she knew it was hopeless to expect anything before morning. Wondering if there would be a morning.

Stock-taking wasn't any too good on this night of brawling trees and she could have sobbed in the shaken dark for the emptiness of the motel room and the cold cream and the re-plays on telly. Joke's over, Miss Klein, she told herself. Joke's way way over. And after one more delaying cigarette she went back into the top-heavy shadows of the veranda to check the water-level. Lamp-light was still showing from the other shack between the scrimmaging branches, and faintly she could hear the pulse of transistor radio expanding and narrowing its fur of static that became, as she listened, the diastole-systole placental force linking her to the only other human within this egg of water.

Her bare toes on the veranda planking became aware of their balancing tensions; the skin on the sole of each poised foot tingled and a current of apprehension shook her whole body as she bent shuddering across the rail to flash her torch on the water below. It was biting the top step. The rain became teeth.

'Leo!' she bawled, quite uselessly against symphonies of squall. 'Leo!' The radio replied in breathy bursts of static and violins. Her third and fourtn cries were slashed off the tip of her tongue and drenched, whatever she meant to tell him. And through the hatred of him, through this last evidence of his soft brutality, unexpected, the wanting sprang contrarily. It made her gulp, wetted her eyes with anger.

Her decision stopped the rocking in her blood.

He had become the desired coefficient, the necessary factor of disaster she craved and detested. Almost calmly now she walked back into the room and by torch-light inspected her face in the small wall-mirror. Doubled, though not what she really hoped for; rather what she dreaded: the face carved more sharply into definiteness in which the eyes, the eyebrows, even the darker stain of her blurred mouth, appeared to be awaiting an answer. She swung her hair forward across those parts of her face which she found harshest and in its loose shadow confidence rose. Slowly, watching her face, she removed her clothes. Her hands touched shoulders, breasts, testing his indifference; and her feelings were mostly hate. I hate him, she insisted aloud. Hate him. Running the heels of her hands down each slow thigh. Hate.

By the veranda edge the torrent was cold and muddy.

One step and she was in to her waist, and then the current grabbed her and flung her towards the bridge. In a minute she had crashed against it and felt the skin above her ribs rip as she hung there just keeping her head gruntingly above water. Inch after inch, using the logs as lever, she shoved her way through a force that delighted her perversely until pummelled, gulping, under the slamming drench of rain, she was snatching at slimy weeds on the far slope, grasping, slipping, losing, dragging, and at last hauling herself through mud and banana ooze onto higher ground.

She took a couple of falls in the beating dark and was filthy with turned earth and plasters of leaves and blood. But the sky streamed over her naked body, a terrible effluence, slapping the hair-licks back from her face as she leant gasping against one of the fruit-trees.

His lamp shone through the movement all about her with the steadiness of truth, of honour. But then she couldn't think for rain.

Out of shelter again and up through the squelch towards light and music. Hatred and wanting were intertwined, had become that moment towards which everything else had built.

A blown passion vine caught her before she reached his stairs and plunged her once more on her face into slush. Something hot zipped in a tendon behind her knee, and when she tried to pull herself up pain shouted her down.

Again she had a vision of herself, an animal vision, as slowly, on all fours now, she crawled up the higher ground the last thirty paces to his shack, unaware of water, pain, or blood; and she laughed, crawling towards that other face in the mirror, knowing nothing most beautifully, her purpose the empty kernel of lit music.

At the foot of his stairs she cried furiously and briefly for her shame, grief and rain becoming one.

Ponderously she dragged herself onto the first step, then the second, before she called out to him.

She heard the movement of his chair shoved back, heard his bare feet pad across board; and not until she felt the frightful quality of him did she look up, forcing herself into the one word, 'Please?': into one smile – the whole body and want of her into one doubtful, querying smile as he looked down at her on all fours, naked, glistening silver with lust and rain.

'That's better,' he said. 'That's more like it. Come on in.'

7

Write Me, Son, Write Me

7

Moth tells me this. And what she doesn't tell Bo does. And what he doesn't tell I see.

She says: Dad was given to such phrases as 'a woman should fruit her loins', a rich unctuous statement of such masculine simplicity his wife had believed him. They had produced an elfin, buck-toothed girl who had entered her teen years on ballet points and had proceeded to give them all the versions of a middle-class hell. They wanted security for her, a go-ahead husband with an expense account and a house that could possibly be marked in the real estate guides with an asterisk – their version of the Trinity. She wanted success without effort (which the education system would surely have provided for her had she stayed with it), scruffy boys with bulging jeans, the pillion seats of motor-bikes, and pot.

At fifteen she was expelled from her convent school for scrawling 'Mother Philomène has it off with the bishop' on the wash-room walls. She vanished overnight with boys.

'Love,' her poor mother told her, 'isn't something you toss around like garbage. Love,' – holding her right hand somewhere on her chest – 'love hurts.'

'Not if you do it right,' her daughter said.

At eighteen she was removed from the back row of a Brisbane ballet company when, convinced by hallucinogenic drugs, she insisted she was the soloist in the only performance of the *Nutcracker* ballet that ever had two sugarplum fairies. She bought herself some cheap Indian frockery, lengths of clacking wooden beads, began to call herself Moth, and vanished into the hills.

When her parents discovered her address they wrote despairing little notes and sometimes she answered. She answered with demands for money. They sent clothes she never wore, and plastic-protected food parcels and once, after a couple of years, she came to visit them with three remarkable others and a tiny boy called Wait-a-while whose parenthood she seemed vague about.

At twenty she was still loosely connected with a large and shambling young man who, like Moth, appeared to have no regular employment though his desperate search for work had taken him to every surf-spot on the eastern seaboard. It would have been difficult to imagine such splendid physique going unwanted by those who needed to employ brawn; but apart from brief periods when a degrading love of survival forced him into well-paid terms as a strike-breaker, he took the dole. He was gentle, had a candid smile and a kind of flecked innocence.

'I can watch,' Bo explained to Moth's parents, allowing Wait-a-while to gnaw on his big harmless thumb, 'the sun come up in the morning. And I can track its progress all day across the sky.'

They were too stunned to discuss the work ethic.

'But how do you eat?'

'We manage.' His paws moved gently across Wait-a-while's fragile shoulders. 'People are kind. You wouldn't believe. And we've given up meat altogether. That's a gas saving, man. We're into fruit. We've rejected all animal products.'

'Has Wait-a-while rejected meat?'

They ignored this. 'We won't be sending him to school,' someone else said. 'We're not going to give him the hang-ups we had, man.'

'Good God!' cried Moth's father. 'Good God! Do you always travel in threes?'

They moved on and north.

There is a hypothetical quality about the aimless mists of early morning rain-forest, a demi-postulation that appealed to the very indeterminateness of their life-style. (I felt it, feel it, but then I belong to an older breed; and despite all that joy, that juice, mister poet man, I'm able to withstand those sensual assaults and stand back a bit, eh? I've always found the trappings of nature to be very soft porn, the landscape's centre-page spread.)

They found others like themselves. They skulked in lean-tos made from iron and timber off-cuts. They twanged out-of-tune guitars, sang their particular rain-forest dirges, got stoned on grass, and each fortnight, responding like children trained by the Jesuits to the vestiges of ritual, hiked in to Mango to pick up their dole cheques.

Dust. Shag-wagons. Blue Kombis.

One of them played flute, I might have told you. Its mournful embroideries would flutter in rags past my office windows and Willy Fourcorners, who now does a little odd-jobbing for me, would look up from his spading to wave, to grin. It looked like the rag-tail of Hamelin as they headed for the road-house, startling the travellers who'd paused for a bottle of soft. Some of the girls made dancing movements, doing their own eyes-down thing, absorbed by the fretwork of their feet on the smudged grass-strip. Moth, who had the edge on them, would dash off a series of *entrechats* between the beat-up tables or hold a tremulous arabesque in the bright sun long enough to catch applause. 'Hey, hey, Moth!' her buddies uttered listlessly. 'Hey! Way out!'

Some months before she had registered with the Reeftown employment office as a teacher of ballet. Reeftown, she felt, was sufficiently remote for work demands never to be made.

The official was fascinated by the small gold ring that decorated Moth's left nostril.

'Can you,' he asked, 'dance?'

'Of course.' She whipped into immediate gambades. The lethargic applicants lining the wall stirred for the first time in days.

'Certificates?' the official asked, ignoring a *grand jeté* that brought her panting slightly to the edge of the counter.

'Not with me.' Moth smiled engagingly and the little ring sparkled. 'I can send for them.'

'Do that,' the official said, checking his tea-break watch, She returned to the rain-forest.

After a month Moth went back down to the coast and returned to the employment office. The loungers were where she had left them. They seemed to have grown a little older.

'I'm not getting any money,' she said. 'I'm starving.'

'You have to wait six weeks.'

'Six weeks?'

'Six.'

'A person could starve!'

'A person could.' He smiled at her quite nicely.

'Any jobs then?'

He hunted out her card and read it slowly. 'Could be.' He looked up at her. 'Could well be.'

'In ballet? I mean ballet? That's all I can do.'

'It so happens,' the employment clerk said deliberately, 'that we have a request for just that. For just very that. Down

town here. Three afternoons a week at a private dancing
school. Payment by the hour.'

He watched interestedly as she went pale.

She told him she lived out of town. She told him she had
no transport.

'But you managed to get here.' He was very gentle.

'Get stuffed!' she said.

There were delays of chequeless bravado during which her
friends, consoled, nourished, advised.

'Longest time I've been employed was a month last year.
Actually I've only had to do three months' work in the last
eighteen. Not bad, eh?' one said. He was plumply in the pink
and given to bib-front overalls above which his seraph smile
challenged the world. 'No hassle. No sweat. Look at it this
way: We're eating, aren't we? We got no problems, have
we? As long as we purchase we're keeping the economy
fluid. Someone pays, hey hey hey!'

But after another six weeks the rest of the commune
became a little weary of her having no money to contribute.
It cut right across community spirit. And at times Wait-a-
while's yowling seemed excessive. Dimly, vaguely, like an
afterthought, she recalled her parents.

Dear folks, went her letter home after memory had
dredged up her address, *I've got it all together up here. The
climate most of the time means relax relax, the family's working
pretty hard at self-sufficiency (guess you city-slickers don't know
what that means, huh?) and we're growing lots of our own stuff.*
She chewed on her pen end and inspected the wilting banana-
tree that cringed away from the door. *But it's tough going
sometimes and most of us are trying for jobs in town but it's like
everywhere I guess there's simply nothing going. Sometimes I feel I*

should have done a typing course like you suggested but who wants that sort of coop-up? Not me. Sun light trees air – we've got it all.

 Well almost all. It's like this Mum and Dad if you can see your way to sending me a little something, the clinking kind I mean to tide me over for a couple of weeks I'd be ever so. We're flat out of fertiliser and stuff and the old agro-eco system (sorry to get so tech!) needs a jolt.

Take care.

 Your Moth child.

 It was three weeks of shag-wagon Kombis and talcum dust before their reply came.

 Darling, they wrote, *we were so happy to hear from you and know you are all right. It's a very long time since we've heard and we weren't even sure of your address. Dad and I would have answered sooner but we've been ever so busy these last weeks painting the old place up (you wouldn't know it! — bamboo beige with chocolate trim) and then the roof developed this terrible leak. I suppose you read about the floods we had last month. Anyway, everything was chaos. So we've had all this enormous expense, what with getting the mud out and the paint and the roof and everything.*

 We're so glad to know you've been thinking about suitable employment. Dad says he'd be only too happy to pay for you to go to business college, but he would like you to do it down here where it would be more practical. Please think about –

 Moth dropped the letter like an unclean tissue onto the floor.

'Oh, shit!' she cried. 'Those mean bastards. Those stinking shit-mean bastards!'

Wait-a-while hooked onto her dangling skirts and worked away with a banana.

'Don't worry,' Bo advised tenderly. 'Don't worry, Moth. No hassles, eh? I'll try my olds.'

He wrote them a postcard because there was less space to fill. He asked for fifty dollars.

It was a long time since he had written and even longer since he had seen them. They still had other children to worry about and wisely assumed their son's sheer largeness was his best protection. Yet now and then, moved by some memento of her eldest in the quirks of her youngest – a puckered grin, the vulnerability of large scabby knees – his mother had sent him soft concerned notes that said, 'Write me, son. Let me know if I can help.' Peering through the brightly lit picture-windows of love, she observed her own unquenchable devotion but believed it to be his.

She wrote at once, a long paragraph of tenderness. She told him about his brothers; she uttered oblique and timid pleas for his return; she worried about his health; she hoped he was able to find a job; she wondered humbly would they see him for Christmas. Also she included a large cheque – and as she gummed down the envelope her youngest child dropped from the tree where he had been terrifying some currawongs and broke his shoulder.

She forgot to post the letter.

It was a month before she remembered, for during that time as well she had discovered a lump in her breast and there had been all the bother of an operation. Her penitence expanded like some monster balloon gassed up with affection as she tore the unposted letter open, added a postscript of contrition and an even larger cheque. She didn't tell him

153

about the lump. 'Write me,' she wrote. 'Tell us how you're getting on.' And she explained his brother's nasty accident.

Each day for that month Bo, who was worrying himself out of the boyish freshness that marked him, foot-padded the four miles into Mango, sometimes with Moth and Wait-a-while, sometimes with a very plump girl who had just joined the family after finding Jesus, sometimes on his own.

Blue Kombis, dust, shag-wagons.

In what passed for winter in this distant north, the landscape became clear, definite, and the canopy of the rain-forest, he observed, trudging along his high ridge, looked like astrakhan across which the shadows lay in wispy layers of blue. He remained care-free; but in the third week Moth ran away to Brisbane with a passing folk-singer who was forming a skiffle band. Absent-mindedly she forgot to take Wait-a-while, who failed to miss her; but unexpectedly Bo pined as he munched on his pumpkin seeds and finally he scrounged a few sheets of paper and wrote.

Dear remembered friend,

I welcome this opportunity to dispense with bullshit say what fond memories I have of you. I can't say that the thought of you being so far away hurts, time was always the best remedy for hurt but I would really dig to hear from you, the cherished memories mean less when I realise how much you'd changed you must have. I still read the old letters you sent me a year ago when you went away P.S. with no returning addresses, remember those days? which stir a fondness which never seem there in old situation. I'm glad you make me realise the affinity I had for you listen kid I want to see your ass back this summer. Funny how a hick town like Mango becomes the other half just because I'm here and converse. So package yourself away from Mister Acne and other city shrinking pains and preserve thyself my child. The best package I seem to find is happy friends that's one thing I wish on you – so if you ever run short remember your own puss is magnificent. Other choice newsy items follow:– Over the last two weeks everyone has grown two weeks. Everybody is a far more interesting thing I'm starting to get a head together making more different friends is what we need most (eh? as someone once wrote me) it's easier now all is less tense pretty big 'adolescent' type problem to conquer!! Pause for a think mind is blank Wait-a-while pretty cool but pining, have been reading Nabokov man just like the old 'tin drum' beat away while I read it does me good also scrape the copper together and get along to see the first Fellini Film you come across man we miss out on so much colour speaking Englisk (said he spelling it with ISK*) How go narcotics down there, not as good as food – I had such a* WOW *time over the last few weeks – dope mescaline music leading into a pill pop party which cooled me off for the present while Heavy Heavy Scene kid it's like whiskey payout or keep dry no inbetween Why do I tell you this What am I doing I hope Brisbane mail has more respect than fucking Mango customs Ho hum long arm of the Queensland law. Well kid? get the picture – saying may head is coming together is sure sign that it aint Bliss to be insane and irrelevant. Give us all the dope, huh, joke!*

There was further silence while Moth in the dry south became the slightest of wing flickers around a twenty-watt bulb.

Bo kept walking the road to town with the dust, the shag-wagons, the blue Kombis. One of the farmers along the river offered him a job, but he only stayed two days, blushed, and told the bloke he had a crook back.

The weather changed. Clouds marshalled their slow-moving ranks up from the coast, nudged the hills, and burst in an apocalypse of water. After, there was calm and penitence, a smidgin of penance during the steady washaway round the piles of the damp humpy where five of them now stared miserably out through the sticky air at Wait-a-while slushing round in the mud beneath the banana suckers. He fell and was covered in slime· and came back inside to complain.

'Cool it, man,' they told him. 'Don't make a heavy scene.'

Bo kept promising the others that the olds had to write. The spirit of the commune was becoming impatient and Bo felt he was a terrible burden.

When the Wet had got into rhythm, when Moth had failed to answer, he trailed one day during a sun-burst, lugging Wait-a-while along the highway slush into town. The corner pub had sculptured arrangements of darkies and despair. There was a further grouping beneath the awning of the old picture hall. It was three days to Christmas and Mango was sweating its expectation. An old Aboriginal woman was squatting on the steps of the hall mulling over her shopping-list aloud with a bent old black man. 'I'll git a poun' a' sausage mince,' she was saying. 'An' tripe. Maybe bitta tripe.'

Bo's rush of pity changed to pain for himself. He wanted to howl. Jesus, he thought, back home they'd be doing the tree and all, and mum cooking herself stupid and chicken and the lot: pudding with sauce and the kids crackling round on wrappings all colours, blowing the squeakers: even the old man mellowed out after a couple of jugs. He gave Wait-a-while a hug that made the kid bellow with surprise, hollering with his mouth stretched wide and a nose that needed wiping. Write to me, mum, Bo was pleading inside. Write. And hugging away at the stringy kid.

Charlie Hanush, the postmaster, was watching through the door; he was an acid cove, filled with the wonder of near-retirement. He moved dedicated and deadly through the paper-work of his days in which each memo was planted square and each day rectangular; and he couldn't stand these bums always coming in bugging him for mail and cheques. His face didn't alter as he watched Wait-a-while yelp for a pee, saw Bo take off the kid's pants and steer the little trickle onto the grass patch.

Bo hauled the kid up the post-office steps, still holding Wait-a-while's pants, and dumped him on the office counter Bo's candid grin was beginning to be muddled by hopelessness.

'Hi, Mr Hanush!'

'Son,' Mr Hanush said, 'get that kid of yours off the counter.'

'Any mail for me?'

'Look, I said to get that kid off, eh? You deaf or something? Don't want any bare bottoms there, see? Not where the public has to use it.'

Bo lifted Wait-a-while from another small frightened puddle.

'Oh, God!' Mr Hanush said. His wife fussed over with a rag.

'Geez,' Bo said. 'Geez, I'm sorry, man. That's a lousy scene.'

'It's a wet scene, son.'

There was a smell of Dettol. A couple of Bo's buddies lounged in the door behind him and started fidgeting near the telegram forms. Bo grinned uneasily.

'I thought this was the high-smile area.'

'What,' Mr Hanush asked, leaning his bitter bones forward in threat, 'can I do for you?'

'Any mail then? I asked. Kimball.'

'Say please.'

Bo sniggered with embarrassment. 'Please,' he said.

Elaborately avoiding the damp patch, Mr Hanush stretched over to the pigeon-holes and took down a wad of mail. Slowly, extra slowly, he began sorting it over, not looking up at Bo's strained face. 'Here,' he grunted after a bit. 'There's one for you.' And he held out a letter to one of Bo's buddies who cackled pleasantly and went down the steps. Bo shuffled his thongs about on the floor. He felt like a dog waiting for – Jesus! even a pat!

Mr Hanush went right down to the bottom of the bundle and then started again from the top. 'Might have missed it.' He gave Bo an ironic smile. 'We can't be too careful, can we?'

Finally he looked up as he extracted a bulky letter from the pile and stared hard into Bo's face.

'Here. One for you.' And he placed it carefully in the circle of wet. 'I was beginning to think you didn't have a pal in the world.'

Bo giggled, wide-eyed. 'Who, me? Me?'

He grabbed the letter.

'And listen, Bo,' Mr Hanush said, 'just get that kid out. We can do without the Wet indoors.'

'Like funny, man!' Bo said, cheeky again. He didn't care. He could recognise his mum's hand. 'Hey hey hey! They've written!'

Dumping Wait-a-while on the top step he ripped open the envelope and opened up the letter. There it was. The cheque. Jee – *sus*! Carelessly he crumpled the letter into a ball, shot it light-heartedly across the footpath into the gaping trash bin and raced down the steps flapping the cheque at his waiting buddies.

'Geez, man!' he cried. 'Geez!' And his eyes filled with tears. 'They've written!'

8

A Man Who Is Tired of Swiper's Creek Is Tired of Life

8

If you were to ask me what makes us different up here – or what makes it different, for that matter – perhaps I could say it's because the place is ruled by the Gang of One.

This is the place where anything screwball is normal and often where what is normal is horrible. Life in the Golden Circle. Chuck the facts together and you get a freak collage landscape where politicians, goodness gracious, my goodness, believe in apartheid; where bomb squads can spend up to an hour defusing a case of mangoes; where we have our own Rapetown one of whose local thugs is accepted resignedly and affectionately as Virge the Ripper.

'It's quite simple,' one of the local aldermen said in his defence. 'A woman's place is in the home. There is nothing finer,' he said, 'than a feminine woman and a mother.'

That's telling 'em! Well, buster, here's to that and here's to the man who said, 'When a man is tired of Swiper's Creek he is tired of life.'

There's always been a lot of sad poetry about the place; and the distances that separate us, I mean the physical distances, are like the verse-breaks in a ballad; and once, once we believed the ballad might never end but go on accumulating its chapters of epic while the refrain, the almost unwordable quality that mortises us together, retained its singular soul. How express the tears of search?

Years ago, balking at the potency of the place, I once tried the New World, the US of A, groping after a Dvorak myth I thought might purge this, erase the Swiper's Creeks of the mind: but Dvorak had been eight decades away from the hamburger ritz and plastic pizazz that threatened with its deep-freeze camouflage to choke me. The transplant did not take.

It wasn't simply the potency of this place I was jibbing at; it was something else as well. I was trying to cut myself off from the home town, the old folks at – my slugabout harmless dad and my desperately fading still with-it mama. Long-time gone now – if time goes, that is, rather than us. I'm inclined to think the only moving is done by us. And another trouble with the New World is it's not easy to get in for any length of absorbing purpose. Not like here where it's gumming up with southerners, people who weren't born here and didn't grow up here but have hopped in for their chop.

Yes. It's a kind of carpet-bagger's paradise.

Which is not the explanation for my presence. As I said before, I like it here; and in the middle of the animal bayings of exploiters I still hear the dying music of this sad poetry.

As a business-man I'm a failure, for the place isn't really working. How do you estimate the profits from an average two guests a week in a town off the beaten track? For most of this year, I suppose, I've been subtracting the interest level of my customers from the deficit and striking some sort of balance; but it really just won't do.

Last week the interest dividends were particularly thin. There was this big meaty upright woman and her silent wacker of a mate, and the only juice I extracted was the fact that Mrs Wacker measured plane distances by noggins. 'It's two beers from Brissy to Townsville,' she announced heartily, 'and then one more to the Top.' She was given to those underplay phrases so dear to our myth: 'After the blow,' she'd say, referring to our worst cyclone in years; or 'Bit of a dry' when she meant no rain in eight.

Or I could tell you about the sandy ex-academic (genuine) who came through last month from crocodile country, stayed a week, and pleaded to work out his board by helping round the place. He had half an ear chewed off, and whether this was the result of his labours before or after his new life I never cared to ask. Middle-ageing, he was only just recovering from his bitterness, and told me one morning as we were frying up the jack-fruit for breakfast that he'd tried real estate (the second oldest profession!) for a while, run a soft-drink factory, organised rackety bus tours, and worked as a bar-hand. Now he's beached in an iron shack up the coast where his books moulder and he spends his days reading and fishing.

'What made you give it up?' I ask. 'The soft cop, I mean.'

'Soft?'

'Well, sorry,' I say. 'Suitable-soft. A university job sounds easier than pulling pints or flogging mangrove acreages.'

'I left,' he tells me, whipping the jack-fruit over with his spatula as if he's been at it for years, 'the morning one of my colleagues said, "This student has an expression problem. And not only that, he has an inability-to-read-the-text-books-attend-classes-and-submit-essays problem. I do think we should take this into consideration and give him his pass!"'

'And did they?'

'Of course. I was developing an ulcer. Oh, my God, don't let's talk about it. That's the first time in three years I've even mentioned it. Getting away. That's the thing. Getting away. What about you?'

He must see there's nothing for me to get away from and, resentful of irony, I tell him this; but he serves me my breakfast with style and there is no irony, I swear, despite our oddly reversed roles and the empty units.

'Change,' he says, his mouth full. 'Change.' He's gobbling away like a pudgy old hen and blinks now and again over the tops of his horn-rims. 'Why don't you shoot up to my place for a bit? I won't apologise, dear chap, for the shackery of it, but I'll be away for a while down south – if only to prove by contrast, of course, that this is the best of all possible worlds. You like fishing?'

Yes, I say. I like fishing. A kind of poetry, too, fishing. And I think along these lines for a little and feel I'd like to write it down some time. If fishing is the poetry of living then maybe the real difference between prose and poetry is that with prose you have to go out to the margins. You take my symbol, of course!

Mac heads south in his camper-van, leaving me with the key to his padlocked humpy and instructions on borrowing a semi-ute he's left back of a pub; and I close shop for a week on the customers I'm never going to have and trundle my inertia north.

So here I am, nudging the equator, and it's so long Crusader Rabbit and the Mutant Lobe from Outer Space!

This place should be irritable and brimming with the befuddled phrasings of its history; but it's a ghost hulk now, swinging lightly on its river moorings, its ports slitted against sun. The main street with its dying pubs, its dying stores, stretches out against the muscle tug of river; and the sad poetry takes over, not for what's left but for what isn't.

In the hot open spaces of the town there's no populace of ghosts; no trace of the trepang fishers, the cedar cutters, the miners, the thousands of yellow men or scraps of half-starved curfewed blacks, the publicans, card-sharpers, pick-pockets, prostitutes, the milky newchums. Yet as the days go by I discover they're all here, all back again in reduced numbers in a town that has budded and swelled and ripened and is now withering on the twig of the blue river; and suddenly I'm sickened with the pointlessness of our passion for growing, begetting, dying – and not a thing to show for it. Once this town panted under a miasma bubbling with gold-light; but it's a waste now, howling for time. Time doesn't move; we do, foot-slogging towards the old three score and ten till the boots split open and there's not even a footprint left of those others who've been beaten by the static character of the world. Time wins out. The place stands still; and if it waits long enough, just blinking now and again in the humid weather, the landscape becomes what it once was.

What's left? Some white-painted rails beside the river, but the mangroves are moving in on them and the northern headland that amusedly watched Cook fothering his ship stares unchanged at the now-empty convent, the joss house, the wizened houses, the two placid monuments quiet in the heart of their stone with that one violent moment of their history. I close my eyes for a second, inept sentimentalist, and across blue water the masts of unhurried ships move continually into light. I open them and there's only a natty launch with a crew-cut dumping a slop-bucket into the tides and a sun-hatted frump holding a line.

The hot roadway holds only me and one other, an old and hobbling parody of myself, left leg bent out at a grotesque right-angle from the hip, for whom each step is a terrible problem in geometry; and as we approach, meet, our silent eyes establish kinship.

Who needs Crusader Rabbit? The Mutant Lobe? There's a story in one of the islands east of here that the spirits of dead natives walk north along the final atoll of the group to their final country, and if you walk that way yourself and meet one of the spirits returning from that taking-off point, death will claim you in the year. Perhaps this, although it's mainland, is simply a reduplication of the ultimate launching-pad of the dream.

Under lamp-light Mac's house takes on meaning.

It's two miles out of town on a south-facing beach cut off from the main road by a tidal lagoon and a creek with lasciviously warm shallows. (I found it easily enough. The barman at the second pub drew a map on the back of his hand between drinks.) Books clutter the place so fully there's barely room for the camp stretcher and the rough sink he has rigged up to the water-tank. I take my tea onto the sand-strip beyond the house into sea-chant and watch the place come alive under its mango-trees and frangipani. Two hundred yards away down the beach there's a twinned kerosene glow from a pup tent where a couple of campers are staying. Not your regular campers – the dusk-cries of kids and straying pups and smell of fried steaks – but a whiskered drop-out I passed on the way in, striding the track in his own darkness, and a girl whom I waded past in the creek. She was standing thigh-deep, her skirts hoicked up, dangling a turnip-shaped net in the slack water, lifting the net dreamily, inspecting and lowering it again. When I spoke she barely raised her head for the space of her half-smile.

Along the beach I can hear their voices blown in ragged word-strips from light to ear. Oh, the lighted houses! The comfort, the mystery of the lighted houses!

I fall asleep drugged by the scent of mangoes.

Have you noticed how houses have their especial qualities of happiness or anger or sheer nothing at all? Mac's house, despite its temporary nature, is filled with the absent man: I find him in scribbled memos on old calendars, on the heart pills he's forgotten to take with him, the wafer of sandsoap dried out on the kitchen window-sill. I understand what made him scribble 'A pox on erudition!' along the shelf where some of his books are stacked, and I track his droppings throughout the morning with delight, right to the page he's ripped from Plato's *Republic* and tacked to the canvas walls of his dunny.

I lean in on his abandoned contentment and suck it in with the thick fleshy smell of the mangoes and the vanishing scent of limes.

Evening.

Just as I settle into a nine o'clock lassitude, thumbing my way along Mac's shelves, the Pup-tents appear at my shadowy door bearing a half-flagon of poisonous red to sweeten the intrusion and discover themselves to me as Carl and Rosebud.

Conversationally it's the same old stuff that I've heard – oh, I've heard before – along the Mango waterways, and I turf them at last into the dark again and listen to the ripe fruit explode on the tin roof.

Day three like they're out of coffee man and I buy them off with a quickpack and flee from them across the creek to the parked ute and drive into town which is, I notice, filled with old folk. You want a list? In the first pub I discover an eighty-year-old joker from the Outer Hebrides who has lived the last five years there in a caravan crammed with the ghosts of relatives he'll never see again; two ageing characters from Minneapolis who are trying to run a carriers' business and sell exhausted pot-plants as a side-line; a middle-aged lady from Perth who conducts gospel sessions; a retired chicken-farmer from Sydney; a rubber-planter from New Guinea.

Beached. The lot of them. Sea-wrack.

And the town is plugged with mangoes. I've never seen so many. They split beneath my foot. They stain my ankle. Their hot yellow perfume dogs me. I see boxes piled with them sitting unclaimed on fence-posts, outside shop doorways, on pub verandas. Even when I drive down to the wharf in the afternoon for a spot of fishing with the characters from Minneapolis, there are two cartons of them rotting in the sun. And as darkness sifts in from the sea the stench of them challenges the salt-breath of the river-mouth.

The pot-planters know what's what! We've been together three hours of idle quietness on the splintered boards of the wharf and they have enough subtlety to invite me to share their catch – not this evening but the next. I like that. Enough is enough is enough of people. But when I reach Mac's shack the Pup-tents are back again as I fry up my catch, and what can I do but share? Mind you, it's not the fish I begrudge; it's the washings of silence and sea-tune that are being fractured so that I indicate early in the piece my lewd and elderly preference for solitariness. Carl's fingers have been scratching the spines of Mac's books. He wants to borrow a couple. I explain they're not mine, but he's oblivious to the protocol that goes with possession.

'Jesus, man!' he protests. 'You've got to be kidding!'

Morning four I discover a couple of blanks on the shelves and realise the floppy screen of Rosebud's caftan has its uses. Down the beach the limp smoke from the Pup-tents' breakfast fire scrawls its indifference as I wonder whether or not to limp my accusations across the beach and confront them amid the incoherent scrub. Wise, I try town instead, hang about the front, the pubs, until it's time to meet my Minneapolis mates.

At six the pub verandas are filling up with the seedy, the old, the sun-blasted discards of the tropics; and here we are, the lot of us, gulping our beers and pushing the conversation across flat decades of memory while the wavering atmospherics of the place suggest another drink and another. Somewhere behind the bar a radio is crackling with pop, but no one is listening; and I notice the fourth time the barman comes over to take our order that there are still faint traces of the map he drew for me on the back of his age-spotted hand.

My Minneapolis pot-planters are just suggesting we go back to their place for that promised meal when I notice across the room that the Pup-tents have come in. Out of place they look with their young bodies and faces in this crowd of old-timers hunched over their drinks. They're sucking nicely at something harmless in long glasses and they're not talking much, merely staring, spaced-out, around the room at the rest of us. I even forget them for a while as we finish off our last drinks, sitting passive and sluggish under the punching light of the bare globes and deadened with smoke; so that it comes with the shock of explosion when Rosebud suddenly springs from her chair, strides across the room and kicks a litter-bin to the floor with a crash. 'Filth!' she yells. 'Filth! Rotten and old and filth!'

The bar goes silent. No one moves. Even the barman is frozen in action with one hand poised to take a bottle from the shelf behind him. Shoving between tables, the girl kicks a smoking stand over and there's a ripping clatter as it screeches its metallic way across concrete. Carl's face bears the smallest of smiles. Then she whacks a third bin to the ground at the feet of the elderly watchers whose faces are blank before her violence and screams again, 'Dying! Old! Rotten! Dying!' and lurches her rage into the street.

When I get back to the shack the Pup-tents are gone and I suppose now they are lugging their packs in search of Eden, still walking into late and later summer.

I'm leaving today. This place is too close to the bone, the me, the ultimate me of me.

I've padlocked Mac's shack and with exaggerated and farewelling care I park his old ute square onto the back fence of the pub while I take one last monochrome snapshot of the town with my good-bye eyes, finding the lens isn't blurred this time as I haul myself onto the makeshift bus that runs out to the air-strip. The driver is a thin courteous socialist fanatic not given to many words, except to tell me he's pulling out of the job in two years and he can't wait for retirement. Where? I ask. And he says here.

We pick up mail and we pull in at the bakery to take up a crate of bread for the plane which will unload it along with its cartons of Courvoisier and toilet paper on one of the tourist islands of the blest south of here; and as I give him a hand I crack my elbow so sharply on the metal edges of the van I'm aware of mortality. Aware. All the way out on the empty road, aware: the lagoon is still under a clotting of water-lilies; the road-house near it advertising steak-night fries and reef-bakes is unpeopled; beside the abandoned brick-works an old cement-mixer is covering itself with vines. When the van drops me off at the waiting-shed there's no one in sight but an old codger dragging a hose along the garden-strip and plunging the nozzle for a brief transfusion into the struggling roots of allamanda and hibiscus.

For ten minutes the sky stays empty and then the little plane appears, miles down the coast but swelling each second till it's dipping, circling, and swinging in for its run down the strip.

The bus goes out to meet it.

At first the plane appears empty, but after a while I see the pilot helping down an old woman, very tiny, very frail. From this distance I see his arm directing her to the shed and slowly, step after tiny step, she shuffles towards me carrying her bulging grandma bag; and I wonder, as I watch her cover painfully that hundred-yard stretch, if it seems like ten miles. After she has struggled to the gate off the tarmac, I see that despite the morning heat she's wearing an old blue cardigan and clutching a straggling afterthought bunch of flowers someone has given her. It's a very tiny bunch. I help her onto the seat. There's no one around. The pilot. The bus driver. The fat old codger running the hose. Me.

She has a pressed and diffident face that's trying to be brave alone at the top of the lost end of the world.

'Is anyone meeting you?' I ask. No one out there seems to care. We really are in limbo.

She's deaf and I try again.

'It's not too hot,' she says and gives a timid bit of a smile, tugging her old cardigan round her.

I repeat my question.

'Can't stand the cold. My daughter, she's gone to Goulburn. It's too cold for me. I love the heat.'

'Do you?' I have to shout it again. 'Do you?'

'Oh, yes. Can't bear that cold.'

I gaze all round me at the empty circle in the scrub. The pilot. The bus driver helping unstack the plane. The old codger. And behind us, beyond this last hoop of reality, the untranslatable idiom of trees and emptiness.

I say more loudly, 'Isn't anyone meeting you?'

She flashes me an old tired look. 'I'm going to the hospital.'

'Hospital?'

'It's a place for old people like. Well, I'm old, aren't I?' she asks defiantly.

On your own! I marvel. Dumped?

'Where's your family then?'

She catches the last words.

'Oh, it was a big one. Six I had. Four boys and two girls. The boys, they're married, all of them, and I got eight grandchildren.'

She nods and in reflex one brittle hand feels for the scraggy flowers that are all that's left of them up here. 'Eight!' Smiling and nodding to herself.

'And your girls?'

'They give me these. The littlest one did.'

'But your daughters? Your girls? What about them?'

'Oh, they're married, too. They're down south. It's too cold for me that place.'

'I suppose you know it up here, then?' I say.

'What's that?'

'I say I suppose you know it up here. Have you been here before?'

'Not here. My daughter was here though. She lived here. She says it's not too cold. She fixed it all for me. Said the heat would do me good.'

'Did she?'

'Yes. She says when she went to Goulburn, "Mum, you won't like it. It's freezing," she said. "I know just the place for you. You won't need your woollies there, eh?"'

The old lady looked across the tarmac into heat glitter that crackled with southern frost and mumbled a little to herself, but I couldn't catch much of it.

'You must have been pretty busy with six,' I say. 'Kept you working.'

'What's that?'

'I said six must have kept you busy.'

She nodded. 'Oh, yes. I was always busy. I used to say I never had the right to be tired.' She gave her little smile again. 'I got the right now, eh?'

'You've got the right.'

172

The bus driver and the pilot were both waving and calling me across to the plane for take-off. It's pretty informal here. That's why I like it.

And then the moment gathered itself into a point. Somehow I couldn't bear to leave her like this in stranger country – but what could I do, what could I say? She sat there tugging her cardigan round her vanishing body and hugging her big dilly bag that looked like her only luggage, that and the little bunch of garden flowers.

'I've got to go now,' I say. 'I hope you had a nice trip up.'

She doesn't hear, but she sees me get up and she sees the pilot walking over to the safety fence calling me, and she is wobbling to her feet again.

'He didn't fly too high,' she says.

I can't bear it.

I tell her again I have to go and she still doesn't hear and there's the smallest touch on my arm when I make to leave, as if something has alighted there no stronger than a breath; and I turn without looking round and limp across the grass past the old bloke with his hose, through the gate, and out into the heat of the air-strip.

But when I'm settled in the plane and look back through the window I see she is coming after me. Slowly. Half-way across the tarmac – and she doesn't really know where to go or what is happening to her. The bus driver is making waving signs from his van, shooing her away and I roar at him through glass 'Let her get on the bloody bus here, will you? Please!' I'm crying. 'Please!'

But he must be a rules man, for he keeps on waving her off; and finally the pilot goes over to her and takes one delicate arm and points her back.

Returned to Mango, the collective inexorable corrupting

motions of the world press in on me and the little journey I had made, supposed to promise change, has become part of the pressure.

I ache like a tooth and I'm not sure whether the ache starts in the heart or the head.

Reply, reply, my questing self demands in unravelling sessions with Fixer (still morose), Willy Fourcorners (folk simples), 'Notes' Galipo (financial plasters), with Brain and Bosie. Brain throbs with crazy advice.

'Migrate. Get yourself a little raft and drift – preferably north. Say you're a refugee from fascism. Deep-seated ineradicable fascism.'

Turn on. Tune in. Drop out. But it's the last piece of that philosophic hogwash I reject. I – want – to tune – *in*.

'Easy,' Tripp says. (Remember Doc. Tripp? Maxie?) 'The problem for most people is they see themselves as total animal – all excitability and want. They forget the other half, the half that accepts its biological mortality. Spirit. Soul, if you like.'

'You sound like Rassini.'

'Not him! He's a professional. You have to come to amateurs for the nitty-gritty.'

I inspect Tripp's face, a haphazard collection of good-natured wrinkles, defined by too much sun. He's shed his last guard along with his practice and his teeth and lives alone in a flash forgotten house on the inlet which his third wife had stuffed with unsuitable furniture and appalling paintings by the artist son of his first marriage. When visitors make social noises asking who did them, he tells them someone broke in.

He walks me down the sloping lawn to the landing where his latest and final wife, fitted out for ghost horizons, swings ligntly on the ruminating tide, aching for the sea.

'Are you looking for oblivion?' he asks. 'Or a place in

memory? Well, you won't get that,' he says. 'It's such a tawdry thing.'

'Being remembered?'

'Being remembered.'

Reeftown is concealed by mangroves. There's no trace at all of Mango skulking in purple hills.

We sit on the rocking deck of his boat and Tripp cartoons, briefly, skilfully, his plans for this year, next year, some time, never. He tells me he'll be leaving next month and sailing north and east, light and easy, and suggests I join him.

'It's not rejection ache you've got. It's acceptance. The bloody ache to accept yourself. The soul part.' He gives me a sly grin. 'That's what they mean by the islands of the blest!'

Birth, marriage, death, re-birth. They're the only neat endings, traditional culminations for living – for books, even – and what bogus back-watering punctuation they are! Living is serial, an unending accretion of alternatives.

As the afternoon sun gutters, I promise I'll join him.

But will I?